Andreï Makine

Born in Krasnoyarsk in Siberia in 1957, Andreï Makine has lived in Paris since 1987. He writes in French, but initially could not find a publisher until he pretended his work had been translated from Russian. Following the publication of *A Hero's Daughter*, *Confessions of a Lapsed Standard-Bearer* and *Once Upon the River Love*, his fourth novel, *Le Testament Français*, became the unprecedented winner of both the Prix Goncourt and Prix Médicis in 1995. Its translation into English by Geoffrey Strachan, published by Sceptre in 1997, also won the Scott Moncrieff Prize.

Since then Andreï Makine has published *The Crime of Olga Arbyelina*, *Requiem for the East*, *A Life's Music*, which won the Grand Prix RTL-Lire, *The Earth and Sky of Jacques Dorme* and *The Woman Who Waited*. His work has received exceptional international acclaim and has been published in forty languages.

~

'Makine is a Romantic: he believes in love and beauty, in the possibility of realising the wonderful richness of life. This makes him an affirmative writer, and one who writes beautifully (once again sensitively translated by Geoffrey Strachan) and with an eye for the most delicate and touching details. But he never shrinks from brutal reality, and leads the reader into a diseased heart of a darkness far more terrible than even Conrad envisaged. His peculiar and remarkable distinction is to be able to look at the worst we are capable of and yet say, "but life need not be like that"' Allan Massie, *Scotsman*

Andreï Makine

Human Love

Translated by Geoffrey Strachan

Originally published in 2006 as *L'amour humain* by Éditions du Seuil,
27 rue Jacob, 75261 Paris Cedex 06, France

This English translation first published in Great Britain in 2008 by Sceptre
An imprint of Hodder & Stoughton
An Hachette Livre UK company

First published in paperback in 2009

1

This book is supported by the French Ministry of Foreign Affairs as part of
the Burgess programme run by the Cultural Department of the French Embassy
in London.

www.frenchbooknews.com

Liberté • Égalité • Fraternité
RÉPUBLIQUE FRANÇAISE

A CIP catalogue record for this title is available from the British Library

ISBN 978 0 340 93678 8

Typeset in Sabon by Palimpsest Book Production Limited,
Grangemouth, Stirlingshire

Printed and bound by Clays Ltd, St Ives plc

Hodder & Stoughton policy is to use papers that are natural, renewable and
recyclable products and made from wood grown in sustainable forests.
The logging and manufacturing processes are expected to conform to
the environmental regulations of the country of origin.

Hodder & Stoughton Ltd
338 Euston Road
London NW1 3BH

www.hodder.co.uk

Translator's Note

Andreï Makine was born and brought up in Russia but *L'amour humain*, like his other novels, was written in French. The action takes place in various parts of the world, including several African countries, Russia and elsewhere. The author includes a number of Russian words in the French text which I have retained in this English translation. These include *shapka* (a fur hat or cap, often with earflaps), *izba* (a traditional wooden house built of logs), *taiga* (the virgin pine forest that spreads across Siberia south of the tundra), *kolkhoznik* (a member of a collective farm in the USSR), *apparatchik* (a member of the Party administration, or *apparat*). Other Russian references include the Nevsky Prospekt, the famous street in St Petersburg (Leningrad under the Soviet Union) and the battle of Borodino, the pyrrhic victory for Napoleon's forces as they advanced on Moscow in 1812.

References to life in Angola under Portuguese colonial rule include *contratados* (men forced into 'contracted' labour) and *assimilado* (a native Angolan granted a degree of civic status.) In post-independence Angola the MPLA (Popular Movement for the Liberation of Angola) formed the first government and was opposed by UNITA (the National Union for the Liberation of Angola) for many years. Patrice Lumumba was one of the founders of the *Mouvement National Congolais* under Belgian rule, became the Prime Minister of the newly independent republic of Congo in 1960, opposed the secession of Katanga, was arrested by his own army and murdered. A number of African cities and towns are named in the text, including Luanda, Dondo, Cabinda, Lucapa and Mavinga (Angola), Kinshasa (Zaire), Brazzaville (Congo), Lusaka (Zambia), Maputo (Mozambique), Mogadishu (Somalia), Addis Ababa (Ethiopia) and Conakry (Guinea).

French political references include the nickname *pasionaria* for a militant female revolutionary and the O.A.S. (*Organisation Armée Secrète*), the French terrorist organization which opposed Algerian independence.

I am indebted to a number of people, in particular the author himself, for advice, assistance and encouragement in the preparation of this translation. To all of them my thanks are due, notably to Christopher Betts, Thompson Bradley, Ludmilla Checkley, Mark Cohen, David Constantine, June Elks, Scott Grant, Don Hill, Pierre Sciama, Claire Squires, Simon Strachan, Susan Strachan, Paul Thompson, Jim Woodhouse and, above all, my editor at Sceptre, Carole Welch.

G.S.

A Masked Child

I

Without the love he felt for that woman, life would have been no more than a night without end in the forests of Lunda Norte on the frontier between Angola and Zaire.

I spent two days in captivity there with a colleague, a Soviet military instructor, and with what we took to be a corpse stretched out on the floor of our prison of dried clay, an African, dressed not in combat kit, like us, but in a dark suit and a white shirt stained brown with blood.

When under threat, our existence is laid bare and we are shocked by the stark simplicity of what drives it. During the hours of my imprisonment I discovered these crude mechanisms: fear erases our purported psychological complexity, then thirst and hunger drive out fear and what remains is the staggering banality of death, the mind recoils, but this reaction soon becomes laughable in the face of the discomfort caused by small bodily needs (such as that, for both of us, of urinating in the presence of a corpse), and ultimately what arrives is disgust with oneself, with this little bubble of being which once considered itself precious in its uniqueness but will burst, along with all the other bubbles.

At nightfall the armed men who had arrested us seized four Zairean peasants, three men and a woman, who were crossing the frontier, bringing food to the 'diggers', as they call the diamond hunters locally. The men were stripped and slaughtered, the woman submitted to their violations with a placidity that lent an almost natural air to the brutality of these couplings. She remained totally silent, not a curse, not a groan. I remember one of the soldiers' faces: the post-coital nausea, the drowsy aggressiveness of his gaze as he incuriously observed the convulsions of the one who had just taken his place between the Zairean woman's broad thighs.

This blasé voyeur now had the urge to manhandle us, it was predictable, carnal fulfilment breeds dissatisfaction. He aimed several kicks at the long corpse of the African. Turning my face away to avoid the flailing boots, I thought I could hear footsteps outside the door, the click of a weapon. The idea of having to die at any minute wrenched a picture out of the darkness as clear as any black and white photograph: the dirty rope hobbling my ankles, the grease stains on the soldier's trousers, the unglazed window opening, very low down in the wall, through which I had just been observing the rapists. A woman's voice, strangely joyful, rang out, cut short by a brief burst from a sub-machine gun. The soldier rushed outside, leaving each of us to his own remission: the African's immobility, the instructor's cough after taking a dose of spirit from a flask concealed in his combat kit, my own thoughts thrown into confusion between this sudden intimacy with death and the pleasure the men had taken in the Zairean woman's plump body.

I was young and this abrupt reduction of life to no more than pleasure and death did me good. It is easier to accept your end when you know you are a piece of flesh fighting to attain physical bliss (like the soldiers outside the window), and dying if it loses. 'Those black UNITA bastards!' the instructor swore. He took another swig and almost immediately began snoring. I admired this man. He knew the raw truth of life. I was in the process of being initiated into his basic wisdom: we're not unique, but all alike and interchangeable, pieces of meat seeking pleasure, suffering and battling against each other to possess women, money and power, all of which are more or less the same thing, and one day losers and winners will be joined together in the perfect equality of putrefaction.

It was not cynicism, I lived these stark truths without really thinking, inhaled them along with the clammy sultriness that oozed over my skin, with the smell of decomposing bodies. The substance of the world was this organic mass, of which we were all a part, myself, the sleeping instructor, the dead African, the soldiers taking it in turns to ejaculate into the woman's tormented vagina, the three peasants with their shattered skulls . . . I felt profoundly at one with this mass of humanity.

'That great fat slob, Savimbi. One day he'll get his face smashed in . . . ideological training . . . for the cadres . . .' The instructor was muttering in his sleep, swatting his face repeatedly to drive away the mosquitoes. I began to doze as well, numb with tiredness, content to dissolve into a stew of anonymous bodies.

The cry that went up outside had nothing impersonal about it. It was appallingly unique in its distress. Someone was being killed. Someone very specific was dying. A woman, that woman, the Zairean woman. I leaped up on my hobbled feet, clung to the narrow rectangle of the window. It was not a particularly cruel sight but eloquent of palpable, precise insanity. A soldier, the big sergeant who had interrogated us the day before, was squatting in front of the Zairean woman, now held on her knees in front of him by two soldiers. He was thrusting his fingers into the woman's mouth, for all the world as if he were a dentist inspecting this gaping oral cavity. An electric torch in the hand of one of the soldiers lit up the sergeant's face. A scar, a broad asterisk, smoothed by time, gleamed on his cheekbone . . .

To avoid tipping over into madness, I tried to invent some explanation, an African rite, an exorcism . . . One of those mythical superstitions the experts delight in, which might have made sense of this nocturnal dumb show. But only one thing seemed clear: the woman had just died and I was witnessing a post-mortem ceremony. A night sticky with humidity and decaying vegetation, the stinging web of insects, these men clasping her body, their fingers thrusting into her mouth, scraping at her throat . . .

The real terror of dying only struck at that moment. A knotty spasm like the awakening of an unknown being which had grown stealthily inside me and was now tearing at my entrails, my brain. The birth of my own cadaver, stuck fast to me, like a double.

After that nocturnal reprieve I was left with the memory of a paralysing panic, then a sleepwalker's exhaustion and then a new alarm provoked by the eruption of voices outside the door, a gunshot in the forest. I crawled along, looking for a breach in the roughcast of the wall, woke the instructor, suggested that we should escape (he muttered, 'This whole damned jungle here's the prison,' before going back to sleep). Thanks to the Zairean woman's death, I was picturing the first moments that would follow my own: the soldiers would drag my lifeless body over and throw it down beside that of the African. The instructor might well be shot as he slept but in any case he was one of that Soviet generation who died in the name of the mother country, of the freedom of fraternal peoples, of proletarian internationalism. On the brink of this last step into the void I felt I was alone. I should have to escape alone.

This survival reflex having banished all shame, I approached the corpse. I wanted to search it, extract anything that might be of use to me: money and his papers, if he had contrived to hide them from the soldiers, any object of value with which to bribe a guard, the pen I could already feel in his pocket. A fine fountain pen, a relic of the civilized world. Its smooth, reassuring weight had the effect on me of an amulet . . .

'There's no ink left in it . . .' The whisper caused the darkness around me to congeal into the density of smoked glass. A few moments later I found I was still holding out the pen, trying to hand it back, like a clumsy and shamefaced thief. 'It's this furnace . . . the ink's all dried up . . . But if you could memorize an address . . .'

I was not surprised to hear him speaking in Russian. At that time, during the '70s, thousands of Africans spoke it. But when I had recovered my wits, what struck me was the address spelled out by the black man. It was a place close to the Siberian village where I was born, a terrain that had always seemed to me to be the most obscure on earth. The man named it without hesitation and it was only the fact that his lips were parched with thirst that added a burning, raw, breathiness to the sound of the syllables. Definitive, like a last wish.

There was no longer any logic to the minutes that went racing by. Everything happened at once. His fevered but amazingly calm eyes shone by the glow of the lighter whose flame I shielded with my hand. I saw his wrists swollen beneath the twists of thick wire that I began to break through, strand by strand. I heard him gasp as the first trickle of water slipped down his throat. We had barely a pint left and, thirsty as he was, I thought he was going to swallow it all. He restrained himself (gritting his teeth) and spoke very softly, banishing my fear in a few words. In the morning, he said, the Cubans would attack and might well set us free. The chances were not great but one could always hope. In that case the two of us, the instructor and I, could hope to be exchanged for UNITA prisoners . . . His tone was expressionless, detached, not seeking to influence me. Quite simply, as I would later understand, it offered me the chance to hold on without fear and trembling. Not to freeze at every cry. His words were there to teach me how to die when it was time to die. For a moment I believed I might be able to join him in this haughty indifference in the face of death. And then I managed to snap the last piece of wire on his left wrist and with his hands free, he took off his jacket, unbuttoned his shirt . . . Before the lighter burned my fingers I had time to see the flesh carved raw, a suppurating crust covered in insects . . . Outside the door a howl from the Zairean woman rang out once more (later on the African would explain to me what the soldiers were looking for in this woman's tormented body).

'Why are they taking so long to kill her?' The thought that formed in me came unbidden. 'They should have killed the lot of us. And, most of all, killed the parasites devouring this black man!' In the darkness I could hear a piece of cloth being rubbed and smell the acrid tang of spirit: the African was cleansing his wound, the instructor had just passed him the flask. Huddled up against the wall, I felt as if I myself were entirely covered in wounds crawling with death . . .

And it was at that moment, heard over the sound of the instructor's breathing (he had dozed off once again), that the African's voice asserted itself, yet more remote than before, not concerned to persuade. He was no longer talking about the likelihood of our being rescued, nor about the Cuban forces advancing from the direction of Lucapa. What he was saying sounded like the murmuring that could be heard from very old men seated beside their *izbas* in my childhood. They would stare into the distance and speak of beings who no longer existed except in their white heads, heavy with years of war and the camps. Elias (I learned his name) was five or six years older than myself, but his voice had a resonance beyond his own life.

He spoke of a train travelling through an endless forest in winter. The journey lasted several days and little by little had blended into the life stories of the passengers, who eventually got to know one another like close kin. They shared food, recounted their past lives, stepped out into snow-covered railway stations and returned carrying great black loaves under their arms. Sometimes the train would come to a halt in the heart of the *taiga*, Elias would open the carriage door, leap out amid the snowdrifts and hand down the woman who had brought him on this trip to the end of the world. They could hear the crunch of footsteps, the hiss of the locomotive in the distance . . . Then silence descended, a constellation glittered above the snow-laden fir trees, the exhalation of the sleeping forest filtered inside their clothes, the woman's hand in his hand became the only source of life in the icy darkness of the universe . . .

He could have promised me a swift rescue by a Cuban commando squad the next morning. Or a stoical, heroic end and survival in the memory of others. Or alternatively a painless death and the future bliss of eternal life. But none of this would have liberated me from fear as completely as did his slow, calm narrative.

The train moved off, he related, and there was a moment of childish anxiety, the fear of not having time to climb on board behind the woman he loved.

Despite the darkness, his tone of voice betrayed a smile and, incredulously, I sensed a smile on my own lips, too.

In my memory the address he had asked me to keep in mind would become the one sure refuge, a place to return to after losing everything, and where you know you will be accepted just as you are.

The door slams shut behind me and the full tragicomedy of the situation is revealed: wanting to avoid the hotel lift and the jovial crowd of the ones I refer to as 'the fat cat Africans of the international conference circuit', I climbed all nine floors of the back stairs on foot. And mistook the exit. Two rooms face onto the roof terrace, mine and the one whose interior I can now see through the broad picture window. I cannot retrace my steps; the emergency exit is blocked, no doubt in the interests of people taking refuge on the rooftops from a fire – so that firemen can pick them up there. And in the room that I can see from the terrace a man and a woman are already embarking on what shows every sign of leading to a sexual encounter. To get back to my own room I should have to walk past their open French window and step over several plants in plastic holders . . . Impossible. I could have done it at the moment when the door slammed: stammered apologies, a rapid dive towards my own room . . . Now several seconds have elapsed, from being an idiot gone astray on the rooftops I have turned into a peeping Tom. The man's fingers are busy between the woman's shoulder blades, fiddling with the fastenings of her bra. We know how to do so few original things with our own bodies . . . His hands appear very black on the woman's milky skin.

I know them: she is one of the organizers of the symposium on 'African Life Stories in Literature' to which I have been invited, he is an artist from Kinshasa. The breasts he has finally liberated look like spheres of mozzarella . . . I crouch behind a plant container, waiting for them to switch off the light and for pleasure to make them drowsy. My own terrace is only four or five steps away. But their lights are still on and their bed faces the French window: if I reached out with my arm I could almost touch the body of the man lying there, whose genitals the woman has begun to kiss . . .

Perhaps it was the expensiveness of their suits that caused me to turn tail. Whenever I find myself among those 'fat cat Africans of the international conference circuit', I am truly amazed at the fine quality of their clothes. Just now outside the lift it was the same astonishment, derived, no doubt, from the years of my ragged youth long ago: 'What does it cost, a suit like that? A thousand dollars? More?' My surprise was not new, but this time I sensed that a reaction was called for . . . I made for the back stairs.

The theme of the conference they are taking part in is sustainable development in Africa (our symposium is no more than a free cultural sideshow tacked onto these weighty deliberations). They had spent the afternoon polishing their terminology: when referring to famine should one speak of 'extreme poverty' or 'absolute poverty'? 'Undernourishment' or 'malnutrition'? A good question, because aid and budgets will hinge on which terms are used . . . Later on, following a protracted dinner, these experts went streaming towards the lifts, laughing with the sibilant and liquid resonance of tipsy

African voices, slapping one another's palms, as if congratulating one another on a good joke. I studied their suits, of the finest wool, and the backs of their heads that sloped down, via rolls of flesh, onto thick necks. I knew that in Africa, more than anywhere else, real life loves the grotesque.

'Malnutrition', 'absolute poverty' and those necks! Even the most fiercely radical journalist would not have dared to invent such a shocking contrast. And yet . . . Imagining these gleaming necks all around me in the lift, multiplied by the mirrors, I felt nauseated, I fled.

And now I am punished, condemned to wait for a sexual act to come to fruition. From my hiding place I can just see the face of the woman crouching on all fours, her eyes are half closed, her lower jaw hangs down, revealing her tongue and teeth . . .

The swift mosaic of memory suddenly brings back the past of twenty-five years ago. A woman raped by soldiers, myself a prisoner, unable to move, waiting . . . The kaleidoscope of life replicates that night long ago in northern Angola but transforms it into farce: a plump female, the organizer of the 'cultural programme', is being serviced by a young painter from Kinshasa for whom she will mount an exhibition in Paris or Brussels. While I am held prisoner between two pots of bougainvilleas. I try to find it funny. History repeats itself, the first time as tragedy, the second as farce. Even our own petty personal histories do it . . .

In the bed the woman is now lying on top of the man, she is the one doing the work, her legs can be seen heaving rhythmically. The panting grows louder, the moment of my release is at hand. I stand up, ready to leap . . . Then the telephone rings, the rules of vaudeville are observed right to the end. The bodies wriggling as they extricate themselves from their embrace, the woman gasping: 'Sh!' Her slight cough as she tries to adopt a plausible tone of voice. Out of breath, she picks up the phone. 'Hello, Christian. Yes, it's me. No, I haven't been running. It's just so hot here. You've no idea. Whew! Apart from that, nothing special to report, really. We're slaving away from dawn till dusk and, as usual, no one's satisfied . . . Is Delphine all right? Put her on. It's Mummy, Delphinette . . . No, sweetheart, I haven't seen any elephants yet. Next time. When you come here with Mummy . . .'

I ran into them at Roissy before the flight. Christian, the husband, who had driven his wife to the airport, reminded me of a certain photograph: a pale, thin man, an old soldier marching along a muddy road. There was an element of old-fashioned ingenuousness in his look, of resignation in that drooping moustache . . . He had their daughter with him, the six-year-old Delphine, and, while waiting at the check-in, he had talked to me about this child, 'a late arrival', and their twenty-two-year-old son. His wife was rushing about in the throng of conference guests, checking tickets, making calls on her mobile phone . . . 'She works like crazy,' Christian said to me, looking at me with his grey, unbearably honest eyes. 'I don't know how she survives . . . All these trips to Africa!' The child, lost in a reverie, was setting out a row of little plastic figures on a bench. Her lips were whispering an inaudible rigmarole. She looked like a little girl from bygone days with her fair pigtail, her lace collar . . .

'I love you, sweetheart. Night night. Let me talk to Daddy . . . Look, Christian, if they haven't made the transfer by the fifteenth, send them a note by recorded delivery and let's see what happens . . . Right. I'll call you tomorrow. I've got a report to write now for the delegate general. Kiss, kiss. Sleep well . . .' She hangs up and remains sitting on the bed for a moment, scratching her shoulder and yawning repeatedly. The man starts fiddling with the remote control, selects a football match, then changes to videos of music with a strong beat. The woman presses against him, kisses his nipples, slides towards his belly. He changes channels. A concert. Handel, I think. The woman lifts her head, her mouth half open. 'The same mouth,' I suddenly say to myself, 'that in a few days' time will be kissing "Delphinette", that little girl with the fair pigtail . . .'

It is hard for the lovemaking to get started again. Desire has run into the sand. The woman swings heavily off the bed, makes her way towards the bathroom. Her bulk had struck me earlier as reminiscent of mozzarella. No. More like soap, very white, very lardy. Or Turkish delight. Her thick, dyed hair is the colour of beetroot. A round face, with little watchful eyes. She is a sow, plain and simple. And yet nothing is simple. Christian, Delphinette . . . The bathroom door closes. The man stands in front of the television. He has gone back to the videos, swaying in imitation of the dancers' apelike antics. I get up, slither in between the thick branches of a shrub, stretch out on my own terrace.

The southern sky. And there, above the harbour, that constellation, Lupus, the Wolf . . .

For a long time the only logic in my life has been the

play of coincidence, sometimes tragic, sometimes comic. As just now, when that memory of twenty-five years ago, a night of great fear in the forests of Lunda Norte, suddenly found its farcical echo: this elegant hotel in an African capital and myself captive outside the French window of a bedroom where a fat white administrator is getting herself seen to by a young black artist . . . He has just stepped outside for a smoke and from my terrace I can see his figure silhouetted against the wall.

In my youth I believed History was set in its path and that our lives ought to be a committed response to this. I thought Good and Evil existed and that the struggle between them in the modern world took the form of the class struggle. And that one should choose sides, help the weak and poor (which was precisely what I believed when, still a young man, I came to Angola) and that one's life, even if unhappy and painful, would then have a justification, and follow a coherent course, structured from one phase to the next. Set down thus, all this seems somewhat naive and yet I lived for years guided by this naivety. And I can no longer even remember at what moment, to put it pompously, I lost faith. The simple truth is that one day what I began to discern behind the great laws of History, the noble causes, the high-flown rhetoric, was the mischievous play of coincidence, a sly, mocking law. For this is the only logic there is: twenty-five years apart a black woman raped by soldiers, a white woman shafted by a black man. And there outside the lift another coincidence, a Congolese diplomat with the smooth trace of an ancient scar on his cheek, like the one on that sergeant's face long ago.

A still more distant recollection comes to mind, that very first image of Africa in a children's book: a dismembered elephant. Its enormous head trampled by a white hunter's boot, the trunk, the feet, the torso, surrounded by smiling and almost naked black men. I remember the unease inspired in me by the thoroughly technical aspect of this butchery. Yes, a great body transformed into a pile of meat, from which everyone will carve himself a slice. Later on Africa itself would often remind me of that great animal cut in pieces by human predators.

'We're launching a programme of subsidy for African illustrators. I'll try to get you included in the project . . .' Now the two lovers are sitting on their terrace. The organizer's voice is languid, lazy, that of a woman physically gratified, eager to please the man who has fulfilled her. I feel the same nausea as earlier outside the lift. And violent disgust, not with these two but with myself. During the session that afternoon I should have stood up and spoken about those suits of theirs or, at least, the fat on their necks. Yes, I should simply have said: 'There will be wars, famines and epidemics on this soil of Africa, gentlemen, for as long as you have those rolls of fat on the backs of your necks . . .' And later I should have walked up to the room next door and said: 'There is in this world, Madame, a six-year-old child, Delphinette, your daughter, whom you will shortly be kissing with the very same lips that are now sucking on this erect black penis . . .'

I smile bitterly. Twenty-five years ago I should have been capable of speaking like that. I still believed in the struggle between Good and Evil. Now this believer no longer exists. The tricks of coincidence are cruel, for they confront us with what we once were and make us realize how little of us is left. There is nothing left in me of the person who in darkness snapped the wires on the wrists of a man on the brink of death. Elias Almeida.

Except, perhaps, this memory, twenty-five years old. At about 2.30 in the morning the noise around our hut fell silent, the soldiers, weary of carousing, raping and partying (I discovered then that war could be a party, too), turned in for the night. Elias stood up and invited me to step outside our prison, as if it had been a holiday villa. He addressed a few firm, calm, trenchant words to the guard pointing his sub-machine gun at us. And the scorn for death in his voice was such that the soldier lowered his gun and remained rooted to the spot. The moon cast a blue luminescence over a few empty crates, an old car wheel and what I at first took to be a pile of rags. It was the body of the Zairean woman. By now I had learned why the soldiers were so intent on rummaging in her mouth.

'You don't know the southern sky yet, my friend,' Elias said to me. 'Look. Up there is my favourite constellation. The Wolf . . .'

The woman held her peace because she had had time to conceal in her mouth a handful of tiny diamonds, given to her by a digger. This traffic in these frontier zones of Lunda Norte is constant. But when the soldiers made to snatch her treasure from her after the rape, she resisted. They killed her and the sergeant retrieved the granules, which were ugly, as rough diamonds often are, without any risk of being bitten.

Elias explained the scenario to me, but, thus demystified, did it become any less harsh, less absurd? Any easier to comprehend?

Nothing was comprehensible that night. Not even the fear. That came later, when I relived those hours in cold blood, giving myself time to be terrified by the idea of one danger or another. And to punish the young man who had set out to strip a corpse, I would exaggerate my cowardice. The shame of having tried to steal that pen was to haunt me for years.

Much more dangerous for us than the soldiers, if the truth be told, was that drunk and drugged youth who from time to time stuck his head in at the window of our hut and threatened us with his gun. He was not a boy soldier, it was at the start of the following decade that those juvenile warriors spread everywhere. No, he was just an orphan, adopted by the unit like a young stray animal. His show of being a little bully boy amused the fighting men. He had picked up an old gas mask, who knows where, and from time to time, as dusk fell, this hideous countenance would appear at our window. The glass in the mask was broken and all that was left of the respirator was a short tube, a kind of sawn-off elephant's trunk. We could see dark eyes, cloudy with alcohol and hemp, a grimace of hatred that would suddenly be transformed into the smile of a weary, sick child. He took aim at us, tossing his extraterrestrial's head, targeting first one, then the other, and uttering a yell that faded away into a long drowsy whisper, then he disappeared. For a time we would hear his howls moving off among the trees. His voice bore a curious resemblance to the high-pitched and desperate tones of the Zairean woman. Two or three times I even thought she was coming back to life again, before realizing my mistake.

For a while I kept an eye on the youth's comings and goings through the camp. He was not there when the soldiers were poking about in the dead woman's mouth. Perhaps he had collapsed somewhere under the trees. He came later, saw the motionless body, doubtless thought the woman was summoning up her strength after being violated or else sleeping. He shook his gun at her to frighten her and assaulted her, imitating the soldiers, grasped her breasts, parted her thighs. And got up again at once, peered at his fingers, holding them up to the light that came from the tents, then to the moon. From the doorway of our hut the soldier guarding us called out to him mockingly. The youth knelt down and began rubbing his hands on the ground. A moment later, rigged out in his mask again, he returned to threaten us at the window more aggressively than before. I was engaged in biting through the rope that bound Elias's ankles. I felt him tensing, as if he had sensed that this time the youth might really shoot. He sat up and spoke very softly, as if remembering a forgotten story. The youth answered him, removed the mask. When he had gone, Elias murmured: 'His father was executed two years ago . . . By our beloved President, Comrade Neto. Whose valiant and faithful servant I am . . . You'll see. Nothing's simple here in Africa.'

All through my life I have encountered Africa experts who could explain everything. I would listen to them, aware of my own ignorance. But the truth is, I have never been able to rid myself of the incomprehension that arose in me that night in Lunda Norte. Perhaps this confusion was also one way of understanding. At least it enabled me to purge my hatred of that drunken child who took aim at me, smiled at me and was quite capable of shooting me to silence the grief that dwelt in him.

In twenty-five years I have found no place among our fine theories for that young human being, who had already raped and killed, and who often peers at me in my dreams through the broken window of his gas mask. No, I have never claimed to understand Africa.

The taste of the wet rope still lingered on my tongue as Elias stood up, teetered and made his way towards the door. I had just freed his ankles. Yes, the taste of the rope, the blood, the tormented flesh. With a few incisive words he waved aside the guard and, tilting his head back, murmured: 'I've always felt this southern sky was very close to us. Perhaps because I was born beneath its stars. Look up there. That's my favourite constellation: the Wolf.'

He must have sensed that in my young head, shattered by Africa, the world was being reduced to the corpse of a woman engorged by the pleasuring of men.

Having arrived during the night, the Cuban units attacked at the first grey light of dawn. At this drowsy and misty hour (as I was to observe one day in a fire-fight at Mavinga) the men who kill and those who are killed resemble ghosts, as they slip away into death it seems less abrupt, a cotton-wool descent, a shape, a life being rubbed out, as if by an eraser.

Excellent fighters, these Cubans! The cordon was watertight, the advance of small commando units, covering one another in turn, was rapid and controlled, like an attacking manoeuvre on a sports field. When their voices could be heard near our prison, Elias called out to them in Spanish. The military instructor, who had woken up, yelled in Russian. The door opened and by the ashen light of dawn reality began to permeate the night's phantasmagoria. Two Soviet military advisers who had taken part in the assault came and joined us. Fresh water had the impact of an antidote. A doctor gave us injections redolent of the sterilized cleanliness of a hospital. The world of the living was reasserting itself, banishing the void. And among the trees the prisoners were burying the dead. The instructor spoke a comical Russo-Hispano-Portuguese lingo to the amusement of the soldiers surrounding him. The spicy aroma of tinned meat hung on the air and gave me a pleasant knot in my stomach.

I saw Elias a little apart, where, under the supervision of a soldier, two prisoners, detailed as gravediggers, were busy. I walked over, glanced into the grave they were filling. At the bottom of the same pit, a woman's body in her torn clothes, one breast bared, riddled with bullets and, pressed up against her, lying on his side in a very lifelike pose of abandon, the youth, still wearing his gas mask. I was on the point of asking them to let me undo the rubber from his face but the rhythmic fall of shovelfuls of reddish earth already covered the two bodies almost completely. 'It doesn't matter,' murmured Elias, and drew me towards the camp. I thought his 'doesn't matter' was a rather hasty way of sparing me a pointless gesture, one pain too many. But as he walked along he added in more resolute tones: 'If there's nothing beyond all this, then men are no more than ants, chewing, copulating and killing one another. In that case nothing matters. And they can bury this kid without removing his carnival toy. Yes. If there's nothing beyond all this . . . To be certain a woman's not just a lump of meat that'll rot beneath the red earth, you need to love well.'

It was perhaps the only time I ever heard the word 'love' on his lips, 'love' in the sense of falling in love, being head over heels in love. Some years later we met in Kinshasa and that evening he told me again about the train that had carried them, him and his beloved, through endless white forests. He was already aware of all that separated them and all that threatened his own life, divided between wars, revolutions and games of espionage. But his voice was serene, almost joyful. He said he would have given everything just for the scent of the cold that clung to the dress of the woman he loved. They were getting back onto the train after a halt in the *taiga* at night and for a few moments, amid the warmth of the compartment, he could detect this fragrance of snow on the grey wool of her dress. 'I would have gone through G-2 again for it,' he murmured, leaning closer and smiling at me. This was the Zairean detention camp where he had been horribly tortured. Men were generally broken there within a few weeks . . . It was then that I thought I understood the 'beyond all this' he had spoken of beside the pit where they were burying the diamond carrier and the masked child. Understood, too, why it was love that made the world matter, without which we should be no more than insects hurrying to take our pleasures, masticate and die . . .

It is the moment of leavetaking on the terrace next door. The lovers arrange to meet tomorrow, to go dancing at Nirvana, the best club in town, according to the artist. The woman, the organizer, has it all planned: 'They'll be reaching the end of their palaver about 8.30. Once I've taken them to the restaurant, I'll slip away . . .' 'They' is us, a dozen writers, the cultural shop window for the international conference on sustainable development in Africa. And 'their palaver' is our symposium tomorrow: 'African Life Stories in Literature'. The lovers kiss and the young man goes off, with a big portfolio under his arm. He had called to show her his drawings . . . Appearances have been maintained.

Only yesterday all this would have seemed totally insignificant to me. A white woman on the wrong side of forty takes advantage of a professional trip to Africa to embark on a not very demanding affair with a young African, sexually better endowed than her husband, Christian, with his honest, melancholy eyes. Being little given to moralizing, I might even have found it rather 'endearing', the gains won by feminism now taken for granted, modernity without complexes. I might have sustained the irony as far as to salute this 'fair exchange', the lady receiving her youth hormone therapy, the young stud support for some phoney association he ran. Yes, I should have had thoughts along those lines, midway between amusement and indifference, and quickly forgotten them.

But many things have happened since yesterday. I have relived that night in Lunda Norte, I have recalled the sight of that youth in his gas mask, first of all the young braggart threatening us, then the child huddled up in a grave of red earth, pressed against a woman with a mutilated breast. I have remembered Elias's words the day he told me about the torture at Camp G-2: 'They hung us from our wrists and twisted our bodies. At a certain moment the pain was such you really felt as if wings were growing between your shoulder blades and they were ripping them off. Then you lost consciousness . . .'

Yes, I had rediscovered Elias Almeida's face and voice in my memory. For long years I had been in flight from this rediscovery, I dreaded it. Now his gaze rests on our life here, myself, the white woman and the black man who have just taken their pleasure and parted.

The woman has showered, gone to bed, scribbled several lines in her notebook (no doubt she writes down the details of all these liaisons she has on her trips to Africa). The day before I should have laughed at it. Now, with Elias's eyes upon us, this I know: while she is dancing with her gigolo tomorrow night, they will be digging a grave to bury a woman with torn breasts and a nameless child. And at the same moment, in a cellar from which no cry escapes, a man hanging by his wrists from a hook will not even feel the burning of the cigarette end stubbed out on his neck by a soldier. Yes, at the same moment. For on this soil of Africa all this happens unremittingly. 'African Life Stories in Literature . . .'

To respond to Elias's voice, one would have to be able to talk about this terrible synchronicity in human lives. To speak of that night in Lunda Norte, the nasty little granules of diamond extracted from a woman's mouth by a soldier just after she had been raped and shot; speak of the asterisk on the soldier's cheek and the rather similar scar on the clean-shaven face of one of the 'fat cat Africans' outside the lift this evening, and of the youth whose left hand, with its slender fingers, was the last thing to disappear beneath the shovelfuls of red earth; speak of the white administrator who, in recognition of services rendered, will arrange an exhibition for her African lover, who draws smiling children; speak of the six-year-old girl, little Delphinette, who does not yet know this aspect of her mother: a tousled head thrust between the thighs of a sweating male; speak of a man whose shoulder blades are being twisted by the strappado till he loses consciousness, feeling he has wings . . . And of that young Angolan in the railway compartment, never taking his eyes off a woman whose dress retains within its folds the fragrance of a forest deep in snow. Speak of this man who loved.

A week after our release I saw Elias again at Luanda airport. The colleague travelling with him addressed him by a name unknown to me. Doubtless one of those names Elias had gone under during his life, or, rather, during his lives. When we were left alone he clapped his hand to his brow and exclaimed: 'There, you see. I'd completely forgotten . . . Here. It's yours. Keep it. There's ink in it now!'

It was the fountain pen I had tried to steal from him . . . This pen would travel through twenty-five years of journeying and oblivion, would several times be confiscated, along with other personal possessions. But I would always succeed in recovering it.

It is with Elias Almeida's old fountain pen that I am currently writing these notes.

II

The bird he had been caring for managed to stay aloft that day, then tumbled down awkwardly. He picked it up and saw in the creature's eye a reflection of the apprehensive joy he felt himself: soon this ball of feathers will go soaring up into the sky!

In 1961 he was eleven. The uprising against the Portuguese had just been crushed. Did he understand what that meant? Did he know that villages had been burned with napalm and that the Americans had supplied the bombers? That impaled human heads were becoming mummified along the roadsides? That to reward the victorious army they had opened brothels into which young Angolan women were crammed, as in a cattle market?

At the age of eleven does one know about or understand and, above all, does one want to understand such adult antics? Elias no longer remembered if the horrors of 1961 had been known to him at the time or recounted to him later by his father's friends. He remembered the bird and its first, hesitant flight.

In any event he knew that his father had fled to the Congo to fight alongside Lumumba, a black man who talked on equal terms with white men. He knew that his father was a hero because he wanted to liberate the *contratados*, the prisoners packed together in lorries covered in wire mesh, on roads scorched by the sun. His father fought so that black people should be able to come freely into the cities where the whites lived, like this city of Dondo, where Elias's mother went to work, leaving at nightfall. After his father had left they, too, had fled from the capital, Luanda, and after long wanderings had ended up in this rotten cluster of shacks, on the banks of the Cuanza, at the edge of the whites' city.

His father was dedicated to the happiness of the people. Elias had heard this from the mouths of men who used to visit their home before the uprising. Less clear was the amount of unhappiness that this great future happiness brought with it. The corpses of Angolans left in the streets by the soldiers. His father's flight. And one night this sobbing, his mother's tears, she who was so strong and cheerful that he believed her incapable of weeping. The hard work in the textile warehouse where she sorted coupons. That was what she had told him . . . But one evening she came home earlier than usual, sat down on the threshold of their hut and looked at her son as if he were an adult. 'I've had enough of those white boozers, their drink, their bad teeth . . .' she murmured, and at once, as if to correct herself, began talking about the days long ago on the island of Cazenga when she used to wait for the fishermen's return. Elias sensed a fault line of untruth in these happy recollections but could not detect what was wrong. His mother was a simple fisherman's daughter, he thought, and his father a man who could read and write and whose features were so fine that people used to think he was of mixed race. Perhaps that could explain it all. His father was fighting for the happiness of the people and his mother was this people, ignorant and fearful . . . Elias felt an urgent longing to be among his father's companions in arms, far away from this hovel with its smell of stagnant water.

Years later, having become a 'professional revolutionary', in the ideological jargon of the time, he would recall that moment when for the first time he had despised the people, with all the arrogance of one who seeks to build a paradise on earth for that very people. And he would reflect that all dictatorships are born of this lofty disdain.

But that evening at Dondo he was too young to be aware of it. Scraps of discordant notions jostled in his head: the flaw of untruth his mother's words had betrayed, the future happiness that demanded so many sacrifices, the time before the uprising, rather a gentle time (as he unwillingly recognized) in their house at Luanda . . . And that baker, a white man, who had one day given him a little bread roll sprinkled with poppy seeds. Elias did not want to count him among all those Portuguese who, according to his father, must be driven out or killed. And his mother's voice, too, now humming the lament generally sung by the *contratados* caged in their lorries. How to unravel all that?

He squatted down and hid his face in a place where all this world of confusion ceased to exist, in the warm, tender crook of his mother's arm. Life flowed on drowsily there, lulled by the pulsing of the blood, an utterly different life, without the grimaces of the dead by the roadsides, without untruth. In the smooth warmth of this arm a scented night reigned that enveloped him completely, his face, his body, his fears. He half opened his eyes and his eyelashes caressed his mother's skin and the folded arm shivered slightly beneath this caress. Happiness like this was simple and needed no explanation, like the coolness that arose from the Cuanza, like the long scattering of stars above the house. Elias sensed on his lips the phrases that would speak of this happiness and the love his face found in the sweetness of the crook of this arm . . . But words seemed pointless. Nothing expressed the joy of that moment better than the tiny stirrings of the bird hidden inside his shirt. Its wings moved softly, tickling him, and from time to time he could feel the minute staccato of its beak against his chest.

Two days later he was already having to run to keep up with his bird's flight. When he stopped, breathless, the bird landed too, then hopped towards him, nestling against his feet. Then he noticed they had crossed the frontier to the whites' city. This alarmed and also amused him: what mad freedom for that frail pair of wings! They would soon be soaring over the forbidden city, even over the river, beating the air of another country, the Congo perhaps . . . Whereas in his case, a few more steps could cost him his life. The patrols shot first and asked questions afterwards, especially at nightfall.

To avoid them, he followed the course of the Cuanza and at one moment had to make his way round a long building resting on piles driven into the sand of the riverbank. Portuguese voices, harsh laughter mingled with the clatter of frying pans, the fierce hissing of oil on overheated metal. The smell of fried fish awoke his hunger. Behind open windows men were eating, draining glasses of dark liquid, calling out to one another, picking their teeth. Mainly white, a few of mixed race, almost all dressed in uniform. Some of them in the company of black women who chuckled and licked fingers glistening with fat, adjusted their hair. There was not a single white woman.

Suddenly Elias saw his mother . . .

The man sitting next to her was a rather small and ugly Portuguese soldier. And this was incomprehensible, for whites are by nature handsome, elegant and incomparably superior to blacks. Elias had never doubted this, as one does not doubt the brilliance of the sun, the currents in rivers. But now the ugliness of this man in his cups was plain for all to see: a crumpled uniform on a squat body, shapeless lips now pressed against the dirty glass, then stretched out into a smile, into a gabble of words . . . And his mother's smile that made her unrecognizable. Ugly . . . And the man's fingers, short, fleshy, gripping his mother's elbow, that thumb thrust into the crook of her arm!

The bird bestirred itself inside his shirt and suddenly escaped, flitting between the piles that supported the building, settled, hidden behind a bush. Elias ran off in hot pursuit amid this petrified forest of timbers covered in algae, stumbled, grazed his forehead against a beam. In the darkness it seemed as if the bird were spying on him, teasing him. He heard its chirruping, moved forward, stooping, then flung himself towards a black ball which was detaching itself from one of the piles.

His hands seized it and at once let go in disgust. It was a dead pigeon, half eaten by rats. He began running again, slithering on heaps of fish scales, on swathes of rubbish. The piles surrounded him, closed in on him, barred his way. He fell and, as he got up, became aware that he was floundering in the waters of the Cuanza, with his feet slowly sinking into the slime. He also realized that he was no longer trying to catch his bird, for the creature had already returned and was obediently perched on his shoulder. No, in his breathless flight he had been trying to reach the row of windows that extended out over the riverbank on a wooden platform. That window, over there, whose support he reached, tugging his feet out of the clay. A moment ago he had seen his mother and the soldier get up from the table, leave the main room, go out onto the balcony. Then a window had lit up . . .

Now inside a little room with yellow walls there was a black woman seated on the bed. Naked and motionless, very upright. In front of her a man was hopping about angrily. The top half of his body was already undressed and he was struggling with his trousers, in which one of his legs had become entangled. His face was very tanned, as were his neck and hands, but his chest and belly appeared white and crumpled. He was performing his leaping dance, hissing oaths. 'Like a monkey . . .' Elias reflected later, while observing that it was generally black people who attracted the comparison. At the time he had been incapable of thought, of understanding. He stared at the motionless woman who resembled a statue of smooth, black wood. She was not looking at the man tangled up in his clothing, nor at the walls of the room, nor the window. Her eyes saw what no one else could see. She did not smile. And her beauty obliterated the rest of the world.

The man finally freed himself of his trousers, stood up, naked on his short, bow legs. Hideous. Went up to the woman, seized her by the forearms, thrust her back onto the bed . . .

The window slipped slowly upwards. Elias felt his feet sinking into the cool mud, up to his ankles, over his ankles. The bird flew off from his shoulder, disappeared among the piles. A boat passed on the river, the voices sounded very close, other voices rang out in response, coming from the shore. The beams of electric torches sliced through the darkness. Footsteps squelched rapidly like suction pumps on the clay of the riverbank . . .

He ran, fell, hid, noticing his shadow projected by a torch onto a wall, a bush. The frontier of the shanty town was very close. He crossed it and collapsed behind a cob wall. In the distance gunshots pierced the night, then silence enveloped him, all he could hear was the beating of his own heart that corresponded strangely to the rhythmic glittering of the stars above his head.

In the morning he observed his mother and saw nothing that looked like that black wooden statue in the yellow room. Only her gaze, perhaps, which sometimes plumbed an abyss other people were unaware of.

He lived through the days that followed in the feverish hope of plunging his face into the warm and tender crook of that arm and thus forgetting all he had seen, causing the building on piles and the hopping man-monkey to vanish . . .

But hardly a week later a friend of his father's came

to see them with a message. From the whispering of the adults Elias learned that Lumumba was dead, his father was on the run and, above all, that they must escape from Dondo as fast as possible.

The warning was late in coming. The next evening, on his return from fishing, Elias found their shack empty. The police had arrested his mother in a street in the city.

For a time his mother's footprints would remain visible in the powdery earth around their house. He would walk with extra care so as not to erase them. Then a shower of rain came and obliterated every trace.

The trick was to walk into the city of the whites carrying an old birdcage. He had found it on a rubbish dump and repaired it with strips of bamboo. The police finally got used to the sight of this young black who, when questioned, would reply: '*Senhor* Oliveira has told me to take his bird to the vet . . .'

He walked past the shopping arcades, the Post Office building, and, hidden behind a tree, began watching the entrance to the prison. At nightfall, when passers-by were few and far between, he climbed into the fork made by two huge branches, hung his birdcage amid the foliage and froze, his gaze hypnotized by the dense crowd behind the high enclosure.

'So human beings can be killed without being deprived of life,' thought Elias, observing this mass of bodies, meagrely covered in rags. No need to drain them of their blood, to dismember them. It was sufficient to starve them, throw women and men, old and young all in together, make them perform their functions in the presence of the others, keep them from washing, forbid them to speak. In fact, to eliminate every sign of their belonging to the human race. A corpse was more alive than them, for a dead man can still be recognized as a man.

The indistinct mass of people moved slowly, trickling across from one wall of the courtyard to the other.

If his mother had appeared at that moment, alone, separate from the cluster of bodies, if he had recognized her, he would have ceased to exist, burned to a cinder with grief. He would have become the cracked base of the tree, the great round stone he put his foot on to climb up . . . Fortunately distance transformed the prisoners into a lava of anonymous cells. And yet this was all he hoped for: to see his mother again.

One evening he again collided with the unstable borderline of life. He ventured as far as the prison gates and through the railings saw a man lying in the courtyard. Still alive, for his arms moved occasionally, his hands slipping slowly across his body. As if he were trying to ascertain on his bare skin the state of the wounds glistening under a restless crowd of insects. 'Worse than death . . .' thought Elias, sensing in his own body, on his own skin, the fire of that swarming death-agony. And he told himself he could not have lived for a moment with such vermin-infested wounds.

The sight of that body corroded by decay turned him into a somnambulist, he wandered away from the railings, picked up his birdcage, began walking slowly, mechanically. He no longer noticed the passers-by, did not seek to avoid the patrols. As vividly as one hallucinating, he pictured his mother beside that half-naked man, his dark wounds buzzing with flies. And told himself that there must surely be a place somewhere on earth where his mother and that prisoner could have taken refuge to keep their sufferings at bay, if only for the duration of a sigh . . . There must be a being who would have offered them shelter . . .

At that hour, Dondo cathedral, massive as a fortress, was empty and silent. Elias heard the echo of his own footfalls on the paved floor and even, it seemed to him, the beating of his own heart, amplified by the height of the nave. So polished was the gilding on the statue of the Virgin that it appeared translucent. He had difficulty in making out the expression on the face amid this glitter, peered at the lowered eyelids, the tartly closed lips . . .

He prayed like a child who had never learned to pray. Only this vision was put into words: 'I want my mother to be sitting there in the doorway of our house in the evening. I want to hide my face in the crook of her arm.' The words, haltingly whispered, sought to convey this to the statue of the woman with lowered eyelids and tart lips . . . He had once seen a film in a cinema in Luanda, in which a man's prayer was granted. It happened in books, as well, he knew . . .

The priest's shout was terse and harsh. Elias jumped to his feet and ran towards the exit, his head bowed to avoid a second blow from the stick. Padre Anibal's cane thumped on the paving stones with an angry clatter that accompanied the fugitive all the way to the creaking of the great door.

Father Anibal was not a hard man. He was quite simply frightened. At this hour each day he passed through the cathedral on his way to meditate in his big presbytery garden. He had already been deep in his reverie when this young black jumped up in front of him. Furthermore, even before taking fright, the priest had sensed an anguished intensity within the empty space of the building, an unaccustomed density amid that air laden with silent prayers, whether ancient or recent. He knew what people generally asked heaven for. On this occasion there was a difference in the vibration left by the unspoken words. And yet the cathedral was empty. He had taken several steps and then stumbled, knocking over a large basket. No, a birdcage! Strident trilling, wings flapping, and, above all, the abrupt movements of this skinny black youth, whom he had at first taken for a lurking dog. He struck out and swore in order to conceal his fear . . . Once he was settled in his garden, his thoughts returned uneasily to the extraordinary tension he had sensed in the nave just now. The bond uniting the one who prays with the one who receives the prayer. And he, the priest, the confidant of both. In his youth he had truly believed in this . . . This evening he did not know what troubled his meditation more, the loss of his faith, eroded over the years by contact with the stupidity and cruelty of human beings, or the face of that child running away with his birdcage under his arm.

Two days later they brought his mother to the house. Elias had no time to think about his prayer being answered, for the woman they deposited on the low bed, like a thing, bore little resemblance to his mother. It was as if a blade had sliced this slender shaving of humanity off that solid mass of prisoners. Her arms, shrunk to the outline of the bones, were no longer black but grey. One of her collarbones was broken and stuck out from beneath a filthy bandage. Her mouth seemed very narrow, greatly extended, on account of the line of dried blood stretching her lips at the corners. The crook of her arm, which Elias touched with his brow, remained cold.

They had got rid of her because the authorities did not want a known opponent's wife to die in prison. After months of massacres they were trying to calm things down, wipe away the blood, portray themselves to international opinion as humanitarians. The Americans, whose aircraft had been bombing insurgent camps several weeks previously, were now beginning to talk about democracy, decolonization . . .

At the end of the second night the bird became frenziedly agitated in its cage. Elias got up, held it in his hands, tried to calm it. But the creature escaped, flew towards the doorway, perched for a moment on the half that stood open, then vanished into the darkness . . . His mother died before sunrise while he was away drawing water from the Cuanza. As the dawn came the river was tinged with pink and it was almost possible to believe that the world existed for the joy of the living.

A week later Father Anibal, accompanied by two seminarists, came looking for Elias. Troubled by the memory of the young African he had driven away with blows of his stick, he decided to repair the damage. Elias listened to the priest's proposals (commands, in fact, which simply had to be obeyed), but his thoughts returned to the pages of a book his mother had read to him long ago in their house in Luanda: a youth who had strayed was set back on the right path by a priest and all at once a radiant horizon of promises opened up before him . . . The next day Elias was admitted to the 'Mission', the boarding school where he would live and study for four years. His own horizon would be the glorious title of *assimilado*. Which signified, as he would very soon learn, that he, a negro, little different from a monkey, could one day gain entry to the whites' world.

He studied ferociously, with the obstinacy of a drug addict forever obliged to increase the dose in order to shut out memories. At his age he already had a whole world of blood and death to forget.

Besides, while he had not yet acquired his title of *assimilado* it was in his interests not to stray too far from the Mission, for once outside it he reverted to being 'a cheeky young African strolling about in the city of the whites'. It was better not to leave the cocoon while preparing, like a pupa, for his metamorphosis into a civilized man.

By the age of fourteen he spoke French and Spanish, in addition to Portuguese, and could read Greek and Latin. He sometimes surprised Father Anibal by quoting from philosophers whom the latter had never read and, occasionally, never even heard of. One day the priest completely lost his temper. They were talking about the history of the Church and Elias alluded to Pope Celestine V, the papal monk who abjured the luxury and pomp his predecessors had surrounded themselves with, a humble man who paid for it with his life. A man who, if he had been living today, would not have tolerated the brazen wealth of some and the poverty of others . . . Father Anibal flew into a rage, waving his stick, Elias even thought he was about to strike him. 'You've been cramming your poor black head with too many things. You've got it all topsy turvy. Celestine is a saint. And the Church needed warriors to bring the word of God to tribes like yours! If we'd not converted you to Christianity you'd still be living in trees!'

He was a hot-tempered man, Elias knew, but one who bore few grudges and quickly repented of his choleric outbursts. The next day, to make up for it, Father Anibal took him to a reception given by the City authorities. In the great hall decked out with Portuguese flags, Elias stood apart from the elegant dresses and colourful uniforms, close to the window, through which the breezes from the Cuanza wafted in. The guests who caught his eye must have wondered whether they were looking at a servant or a youth of mixed race who had come with his white progenitor. 'They've noted that I no longer have my monkey's tail,' thought Elias with a smile. 'And they're telling themselves that in a few more years I may have learned how to eat with a fork . . .'

Watching the coming and going of uniforms, he remembered the yellow room in the long building on piles. It was probably one of these military men who had gone there on a certain evening to couple with a beautiful black woman. The white women among the guests were mainly short and thin, or else extremely fat, in which case they complained noisily about the climate. Each and every one of them clasped her glass in a particular hold that amazed him: reminiscent of a raptor's talons, a firm, voracious grip. He reflected that to get to where they had got to in life, they had doubtless needed to be endowed with these tough, claw-like finger-joints . . . There were also some people of mixed race in the company. They were dressed with greater care than the whites and seemed continually on the alert. They practically stood to attention when spoken to and replied in a Portuguese so correct that it lacked all savour, articulating every syllable as people do after being cured of a stammer.

'And that's the best that could ever happen to me,' thought Elias, as he studied their smooth, rigid faces, their uneasy eyes. Yes, with superhuman application, and by means of countless acts of servility and hypocrisy, he had a fair chance of joining the envied ranks of the people of mixed race. Of living in constant concern about losing his status and sinking back to the level of a negro, about having to be whiter than a white.

That evening, after the reception, Father Anibal honoured him by inviting him to his garden. They sat in wicker armchairs with cups of tea in their hands. The Father was in an excellent mood, that of a jovial parish priest who has drunk good wine, attended a fashionable gathering and been appreciated for his eloquence. 'You see,' he was saying to Elias, 'God so loves His creatures that He even allows them to commit evil. Yes. So great is God's love, that He even grants them this freedom. And that's why wars, famines and crimes occur . . .' He doubtless regretted losing his temper the day before and now wanted to show off his doctrinal skills. As he talked about the wars and famines tolerated by God he had a benign and dreamy air.

'I could become a priest, too,' Elias said to himself. And he pictured a fine presbytery, a garden like this one, ablaze with bougainvilleas but, most of all, this serenity:

nothing happens here that is not the Lord's will. Then he suddenly knew that this God was hateful to him because he allowed his creatures to smash a woman's collarbone. That slender broken collarbone was enough for him to reject this world and its creator!

Elias felt this so violently, choking on such a sob in his throat, that the priest, who had just fallen asleep in his armchair, woke up, as if the consistency of the air had changed. He shook himself, yawned, patted his dog, which had come to rub itself against his knees. 'My old friend Boko's been limping for the past couple of days. Take him to the vet tomorrow, all right?'

The police stopped Elias very close to the house of Antonio Carvalho, the vet. He had to explain himself. As he continued on his way Elias remarked to himself, with that sharp irony which would greatly assist him in life: 'Boko's an *assimilado* already . . .'

The state of the dog's health necessitated an extended course of treatment with injections twice a week. The priest accepted this version in good faith. Elias would call on the vet, leave Boko to run about in the garden and, with a pounding heart, settle down to listen to this strange white man, this Portuguese who wanted to change the world. Carvalho was married to an Angolan woman, not all that unusual a situation for a colonial. What was unusual was that he had not made a servant of his black wife. 'You see, Elias, she's the one who welcomes us into her country, not the other way round. One day the whites will have to understand this. Yes, we need a real revolution in people's minds . . .'

It was at his house that Elias read the works of Marx

for the first time. And believed he had found in them what he had grievously lacked: the certainty that the world of human beings was neither predestined nor irremediable and that it was therefore possible to transform it, make it better, root out the evil from it. One could erase from this world the room with yellow walls where an ugly, naked man hopped up and down before a woman who sold him her body for the price of a meal. In this transfigured world a man covered in dark wounds would not be left out in the middle of a prison courtyard crammed with human ghosts. And there would not be a woman's slender, fragile collarbone, smashed by a soldier's boot . . . Years later he would study Marx in Moscow, arguing about it with his comrades. But his first reading would remain the most vivid, thanks to this promise of a fight against the evil that God tolerates.

Carvalho had known Elias's father but there was a serious ideological difference between them. The vet maintained that, according to Lenin, revolution could not lead to victory without a revolutionary situation being created in advance. It was therefore necessary to wait, to prepare the ground, to raise the political consciousness of the masses. Whereas his father followed a voluntarist line advocated by Trotsky, hoping to conquer with the help of a small group of revolutionaries cut off from the people. Lenin called this strategy the 'infantile disorder of leftism . . .'

One secret confided in him made a much greater impression on Elias than all these theoretical distinctions: Carvalho remained in touch with his father's comrades and from time to time was visited by his contact agents.

* * *

At the start of the following year, 1965, one of these spent several days in hiding at the vet's house. Elias met him and heard an account of their struggle in the eastern Congo. During the course of two sleepless nights he took his decision: he would leave with this man to join his father's companions. He could no longer wait for the famous 'revolutionary situation' to deign to arrive. For the revolution's heart was already beating somewhere in the darkness of the Congolese jungle.

'The revolution's heart', 'the darkness' . . . He was fifteen and it was in such terms that he pictured the world. But, most of all, he wanted his father to know how his mother had died.

III

So here was where the revolution's heart was beating: in this village of the eastern Congo in the Kivu hills. Before his arrival there, Elias had pictured the clash of arms, faces etched by combat, fiery speeches, heroism and sacrifice, words whispered on the brink of death, warriors with proud, manly features. The revolution . . .

The first thing he saw bore no resemblance to any of that. Two women were preparing the meal in front of a hut, placidly arguing all the time, kneading the dough on the bare plank of the table. Their language was unknown to him and this made the scene even more commonplace, it would have been the same in Angola or anywhere else, whatever the country, whatever the language. One of the women was big and mature, very fleshy. Her large, almost bare, breasts smeared with flour, swung heavily over the table, colliding with one another at each movement of her arms. The other was very young, with a smooth body and lithe buttocks. There was washing hung out on a line to dry, an almost homely mixture of men's shirts, towels, women's under-wear . . .

Numb with exhaustion after a long journey, Elias wandered about with the feeling that he had penetrated behind the scenes of the revolution, just where its actors were preparing to perform brave deeds, glorious feats of arms. In the alfresco canteen a soldier was asleep, seated at a table, his head resting on the thick planks where a stripped Kalashnikov lay spread out. One of the parts had tumbled onto the ground. Elias picked it up and set it down discreetly amid the rest of the military meccano . . . Another, stationed amid the bushes, was haranguing his audience. Elias drew closer to listen to him and saw that the orator had no one in front of him. He was addressing empty space, his vacuous gaze floated in a cloud of aromatic, slightly acrid smoke. The same, thought Elias, as used to swirl around the children of the streets, the little hemp smokers, in Dondo's shanty town in the evenings. A young warrior crossed the courtyard with a firmly resolute tread, adjusting a sub-machine gun on his shoulder, as if at any moment he were about to join battle, then stopped, began chatting with the two cooks and laughing . . .

Life in this backyard of the revolution seemed like a game Elias could not yet make sense of. They had told him his father was due to return the following morning and he would doubtless be able to explain these relaxed rebels' extraordinary way of life. Elias had already noticed a whole host of oddities: the drugged orator's harangue, the young sub-machine gunner's unexpected laughter . . . And at night, in the room next door, the ponderous wrestling of copulating bodies, an utterly banal activity, so little in harmony with the passionate purity he associated with the revolution. By the full moon's phosphorescent light he could see the end of a bedstead and two pairs of feet. The movements of the soles of the feet reflected the pleasure taken. At one moment the man's right foot was waving wildly and dug a hole in the mattress. It was ridiculous. 'Pleasure is ridiculous when there's no other bond between us,' thought Elias. The toes curled, as if in a fit of cramp, then relaxed. The foot expressed everything, from feverish desire to final collapse. The woman was the fat cook he had seen on arrival. He was old enough to sense that, among so many men on their own, the presence of such women was inevitable. But he could not understand why the dream of revolution had not yet taught these men and women to pursue a love different in kind from this brief, breathless jiggling.

Many years later he would recall the naivety of the question, while telling himself that this boyish view of revolution and love had not been all that foolish. For what is the point of such liberating turmoil if it does not radically change the way we understand and love our fellow human beings? Then he would realize that ever since that night of the full moon, love had become a secret yardstick for him, a touchstone by which to judge all human activity on this earth.

At first Elias thought a thief had arrived: amid the mists of the small hours a man skirted the neighbouring hut, pushed open the door discreetly, then stepped outside again and studied himself in the rectangle of mirror fixed beside the door frame. He smoothed his hair, adjusted the collar of his combat kit, turned round . . .

Elias recognized his father. He struck him as small ('It's because I've grown,' thought Elias) and dressed with the ladykiller elegance affected by some military men. His uniform was too tight, overloaded with pockets

and buttons. He looked like . . . a Portuguese officer!
Elias moved away from the window, hoping his own
words could sweep away this painful first impression.
He had so much to tell this man.

He wanted to talk to him about his mother in the
prison at Dondo. An invisible woman, impossible to
make out amid the throng of prisoners. And then,
snatched away from that human mass, a mute shadow
lying there in their shack on the banks of the Cuanza.
And beneath her ashen skin, the white gleam of the
broken collarbone. He would talk, too, about Anibal,
the priest whose god calmly accepted it all, this broken
collarbone, a prisoner's body covered in wounds crawling
with insects and the death of this woman who, a few
days earlier, had held all the happiness in the world in
the crook of her arm . . .

He broke away from his father's embrace and stammered: 'You know. Mother's . . . dead. And when she
was . . .' 'Yes, yes, they told me,' his father hastened to
reply and walked over to straighten a map that hung
on the wall. 'Yes, I heard . . . Yes. That's . . .' Elias was
expecting: 'That's terrible,' but his father gave a cough
and concluded, with a sigh: 'That's how it is.'

At that moment a woman came into the room. Tall
and thin. A white woman. 'Let me introduce you,' said
his father. 'Elias. Jacqueline.' She had colourless eyes,
a somewhat lined, angular face, and wore a military
garb of the same slightly theatrical cut as his father's
uniform. Listening to her, Elias learned she was Belgian,
a militant anti-colonialist and internationalist (she
emphasized her commitment insistently in almost every
sentence). All this was doubtless very important but,

58

strangely, Elias was mainly thinking about the woman's long body, which his father doubtless held in his arms at night. He felt a sad satisfaction now at not having spoken about his mother, about her broken collar-bone . . .

'He doesn't look too bright, your boy. I'll have to give him a bit of a jolt. Wake his ideas up . . .' Jacqueline said it in French, so as not to be understood, his father nodded agreement, with a complicit smile. Elias replied in French, looking her straight in the eye: 'Don't waste your time, Madame. The Portuguese have already performed that thankless task . . .' The arrival of another white person rescued the adults from their confusion. Elias had time to notice that the map on the wall was of New Zealand. He never discovered why.

Elias took an immediate liking to the man who had just walked in. Perhaps because he came as close as possible to an adolescent's image of a revolutionary. A face lit by a hidden fire, brisk, firm gestures, words capable of causing his listeners' chests to swell. And that prophetic gaze, faintly squinting eyes that seemed to see beyond the disappointing present, beyond this scattering of huts among the trees, beyond the laundry gently rippling on a line. He was dark, with the long, gleaming hair of a painter and, as he smoked, he released long, curling, blueish strands from his mouth, very different from those emitted by the others, it was his signature in the air. Elias came under his spell, as everyone did. The soldiers called him *Commandante*. His father and Jacqueline, 'Ernesto'. After five minutes of conversation he turned to Elias and proclaimed in inspired, solemn, almost prophetic tones: 'Elias, you will come to us, to Havana. You will study there. You will learn the science of Revolution!' Was it the resonant impact of the Spanish or the ringing tones of the promise? It carried such conviction that, as if hypno- tized, Elias pictured a town beside the sea and a double of Ernesto instructing him in revolution. The Cuban was a kind of sorcerer, a wizard with words, Elias would think later. He left the room, drugged with hope.

This narcotic effect overwhelmed the whole of that little revolutionary base and lasted for two days until Ernesto's departure. The warriors who only the previous day had been wandering around aimlessly or sleeping, marched about as if on parade, took part in tactical exercises, river crossings . . . Even the expressions on their faces changed. In this remote corner of the trop- ical rainforest, Ernesto gave them a glimpse of a radiant path, a horizon to aim for. The speech he delivered spoke of just this horizon, a world of liberty, of plenty, of happiness. To reach it they must take the road of armed struggle, proletarian solidarity . . . Did they all understand this? Elias was not sure that they did but he sensed it was more a matter of magic than of logic. Like the language of sorcerers, he thought, no one under- stands it but no one is immune to it. 'The triumph of our struggle will sound the death knell for the forces of imperialism . . . Your children will live in a world without poverty, without exploitation . . .' The music of these words blended with the shades of night, with the glittering of the first stars. Ernesto's face, lit by the firelight, seemed to reflect the shining future he could already discern in the depths of the forest.

That night Elias noticed a light burning in the hut that served as 'command post'. An oil lamp, Ernesto's head bowed over a notepad, a pen quivering in his hand. Every now and then the man raised his head and smiled, peering for a long time into the darkness. With all the enthusiasm of youth, Elias felt he was living through a moment that belonged to History.

The next day Elias came upon a soldier who was preparing to play his part in History: half recumbent, his back propped up against the hot wall of a hut, he was rubbing away energetically at a smooth, black object. It was an amulet, yes, a lucky mascot, he explained. Vaguely at first, then, flattered by the boy's interest, he was more specific: 'I wear it here, next to my heart. That side says if I shoot, I kill my enemy. This side says, if he shoots, the bullets bounce off me. I've already tried it . . .' He was buffing his gri-gri with a piece of stuff that gave off a greasy, fleshy, stink. 'So that's leather, is it?' asked Elias. The soldier suddenly flew into a rage and thrust him aside, abusing him. 'You shall never know!' he shouted. 'Or else you will die! Never!' And walked off into the forest without pausing in his polishing.

Returning to the camp, Elias came upon a conversation in a dark spot between the younger woman cook and a soldier he had seen before, the one who had been haranguing a crowd of ghosts in a drugged state. Now he was talking very softly, very fast, all the while attempting to thrust a bundle of cloth into the young woman's hands. This was a very fine dress, he assured her, trimmed with lace and glass beads. It was clear to

Elias that they had already reached the final round of the negotiations: the cook was no longer saying no, the soldier was talking with the excitement of someone who is certain his bid will succeed . . . Before going to sleep Elias thought about this couple, who were now engaged in making love. The man was very fat, his belly spilled out over his belt. One had to imagine this swollen, sweating mass pressing down on the young woman's very slender body. Elias experienced a violent constriction in his lungs. Jealousy; desire, no doubt; pity; but, most of all, incomprehension: this piece of fabric with its glass-bead trimmings, this coupling and then nothing, a void, life continuing as before, just as dull, just as stupid. He made an effort to salvage the residue of love in this encounter between a fat body and a slim one. Then he remembered the movements made by the feet of lovers in the sexual act. Tensing, scratching, relaxing. If only he could ask Ernesto: 'Could your struggle one day awaken something other than that in human hearts?'

Two days later he managed to join his father, whose travels across the country he was now to share. 'It's no good waiting passively for the revolutionary situation to arise,' Ernesto declared, addressing the rebels. 'You have to provoke it. Yes. By force of arms!' Elias thought he had heard this terminology somewhere before. But most of all what these words silenced in him was the only question he longed to ask: 'After the revolution do you think people will love one another in a different way?'

He no longer remembered precisely when the spell created by Ernesto's speeches was broken. Perhaps this was the evening: from his seat beneath a tree Elias saw a young soldier drawing a spider's web of signs on the earth with a fragment of wood, smiling at his own thoughts. Lost in his daydream, he was deaf to the orator's ringing words. The struggle against imperialism, the promise of happiness after the triumph of the revolution . . . The soldier already seemed happy here, in this night cloudy with heat, in front of the arabesques he was tracing, expressive of a secret joy, of hopes at once fanciful and humble. Then Elias noticed that the young man was not the only one to be inattentive.

Yet his father, Jacqueline and Ernesto were unsparing of themselves as they travelled back and forth across the eastern Congo, their assigned territory. 'The thunder of the people's revolt can already be heard!' the Cuban declaimed one day at one of the rebel bases. A heavy clatter of cooking pots suddenly erupted from the kitchen, as if in echo of his words. Tickled by this droll coincidence, the warriors burst out laughing. It took Ernesto some time to regain control of his audience, to reimpose the radiant trance to which his flock generally succumbed.

As the days went by the effect of this verbal intoxication grew weaker. One evening, following the speech, a soldier remained in his place after his comrades had dispersed. His eyes half closed, lulled by the drug, he was gabbling snatches of the phrases that he had just heard: 'Marx', 'class struggle', 'neocolonialism', 'Lenin' . . . For him these words had the same impact as the magic formulae intoned by a holy man.

Their forays now reminded Elias of trying to light a fire with damp matches. The flame flickered for the space of a slogan, only to be dissipated by the narcotic fumes in which the warriors immersed themselves every evening after a day's march or a fire-fight. A conflagration would have been needed, the uprising of a whole population, a 'revolutionary situation'. But the revolution was slow in coming and one morning the people appeared in the person of a tall old man who came to the camp and sat down beside the door of the 'command post'. Ernesto emerged, followed by Elias's father, the old man addressed them. They did not understand his dialect, a soldier came up and, in some embarrassment, translated.

'He's complaining because our men have taken his food supplies . . .'

'Tell him our fighters are paying with their blood for the bread the people give them,' declared Ernesto in ringing tones, adding, more softly, for my father's ears: 'There you are, you see. The peasantry is a weak link in the revolution. Always this filthy petty proprietor's reflex . . .'

'He says his son has been killed,' continued the interpreter. 'And now he has his three grandchildren to feed.'

'Our soldiers may die tomorrow defending him against

his oppressors! And all he can think about is his wretched potatoes . . .'

'He says the children may die today . . .'

There were, Elias noted, two peoples: one of them, glorified in speeches, the 'working masses', whose triumphal entry into the paradise of communism was being prepared for, an ideal people, as it were, and then this other people, which thanks to its humdrum destitution brought dishonour to the great revolutionary project.

The warriors, too, were far from ideal. Ernesto used to mark the most exalted moments in his harangues with an abrupt gesture: he would tilt his head back, his eyes fixed on the horizon, as if he could already see the luminous advent of the future. It was just this brief pause that a soldier took advantage of one evening, to ask, in a slightly disdainful voice: 'What about our pay, *Commandante*? When are we going to get it?' Elias looked round. A young, powerfully built man, wearing a new khaki uniform, very different from those the others had managed to procure for themselves. He was surrounded by a group who looked as if they were his henchmen. Elias had a simple and disconcerting thought: 'That fellow in khaki could easily go over to the enemy if he were offered more . . .'

Before going to bed he saw Ernesto writing in his notebook by the light of an oil lamp.

The following morning, on the way to another rebel camp, the Cuban gave vent to his fury: 'For that politically immature soldier to be worrying about his pay is, at least, comprehensible. But when a chief like Soumialot wants to be paid for every skirmish, it's enough to disgust you with this country. And in dollars, too, if you please. And after I've promised him Cuban regiments will be coming soon . . . And our other strategist, this Gbenye. Have you heard his reasoning? He wants to know what tribe the enemy soldiers belong to. That's how he'll decide whether or not to fight. Try talking to them about proletarian internationalism!'

Jacqueline shared Ernesto's anger. Elias's father was silent. Then, unable to contain himself, began to defend these former peasants, now turned revolutionaries. He explained that the country had recently emerged from long decades of oppression, with no elites, with no real identity, and that the local chiefs held fast to the only certain bond: tribal membership.

One day the debate got out of control. 'I'm beginning to wonder,' Ernesto exclaimed furiously, 'whether this historical backwardness the Congolese suffer from can ever be made up. Yes, comrade. I ask myself if they can really be made to progress to the Marxist-Leninist view of the world. Don't be angry, but I have grave doubts over the possibility of ever getting anything into these people's skulls other than drugs, fucking and the sorcerers' mumbo-jumbo!' Elias thought his father was about to reply with equal sharpness. But the man held his peace and it was only after a moment that he riposted in a calm, weary voice: 'Very sorry, Ernesto. This is the only people we have to offer you . . .'

That evening Elias witnessed a scene that appeared to prove the Cuban right. In an absurd replay, he came upon a couple negotiating a sexual deal. Beneath a lamp which lit the entrance to the camp a soldier was holding out a garment to a young woman, all the while whispering a hurried gabble of promises. She was pretending to refuse him but, in her curiosity, was already examining the fabric, turning it towards the light. 'What are these stains?' she exclaimed suddenly. 'Blood?' Uneasy, the soldier assumed a casual tone of voice: 'Oh, that's nothing. It's juice. Or paint. It'll come out in the wash . . .' As Elias continued on his way he thought about the person who had been robbed of that dress, he pictured a woman violated, wounded, staining the fabric with her blood. A woman who had probably been killed for the sake of this booty . . . The Cuban's words struck him as amply justified.

He had high hopes of the first battle he was due to take part in. Ernesto had announced an assault on a base held by Belgian mercenaries. Elias pictured himself bringing up ammunition to the fighters, assisting soldiers riddled with bullet wounds, and strolling around after the battle with a red-stained bandage about his brow . . . But, crucially, he would come face to face with the white imperialists taken prisoner by the rebels.

When it was all over there was not a single 'Belgian mercenary' among the vanquished. A vast number of wounded and dead, all black. 'Africans killed by other Africans!' Elias said to himself in a hard voice, which did not belong to him and which frightened him. To silence it he hastened to assist the nurses, carried water, walked through the conquered village looking for survivors. The injuries did not resemble the noble wounds he had pictured being delicately dressed by women's hands. This was flesh, hideously torn to pieces by fragments from grenades, intestines spilling out from torn bellies, skulls smashed open to expose their bloody contents. Moving on from the carnage, Elias found himself in a yard and saw someone he at first took to be a wounded man shuddering with spasms of pain. The light was fading and it took him a moment to understand: at the edge of a pond a soldier was having his way with a woman, who lay with her face against the earth. He was thrashing about on top of her and to stop her from crying out, was pressing her head into the slime of the pool . . . In the centre of one of the nearby huts Elias discovered a little girl who had managed to squeeze her body underneath a tiny table like a contortionist. She was shaking so much the furniture looked alive. A boy older than her had hidden himself behind a pile of branches. This screen could be seen through but the youth, crazed with fear, must have thought he was rendered invisible by the narrow basket he had put over his head. Through the wickerwork Elias could see motionless, staring eyes.

That night the soldiers celebrated their victory. To begin with they listened to Ernesto but very soon the mood changed. Catcalls rang out, someone fired in the air, bottles of drink circulated. In an hour's time half the huts were on fire and the ruddy glow of the flames picked out in the darkness now a drinker's tilted head, now a brawl, sometimes the excited stampeding of half-naked men around a woman who was being raped . . .

Ernesto, Jacqueline and Elias's father had taken refuge in the village's 'command post', each trying to hide their fear in their own way. Ernesto was writing notes, his father was studying a large-scale map, Jacqueline was pretending to read. But each of them, Elias could see, had a gun within reach, they all knew that from one minute to the next the savagery that was being unleashed outside could engulf them. At one moment a shrill cry, a woman's voice, cut through the uproar. The besieged occupants of the 'command post' looked up. Elias's eyes met his father's. 'I'll go,' said his father. But Jacqueline leaped up, and clung to him, exclaiming: 'No. You're not going out! They're coming for us. They're going to kill us all. They'll cut our throats. They're savages!' Ernesto sat there, holding his head in his hands, his face distraught.

During the night the fire died down and, as if in response to the calming of the flames, the noise of the orgy gradually fell quiet. Elias opened the door. In the sky, star-studded beauty. From the earth an acrid stench, a mixture of blood, vomit, charred meat, sweat, sperm . . .

He could not sleep, thinking about the error Ernesto had committed. The Cuban promised these men a prudent, logical, patiently constructed happiness. The dream of an ideal society, communism. But they, for their part, knew a much more immediate and violent ecstasy: this night, after a battle, the exaltation of drink and drugs, the absolute freedom they had to satisfy any desire whatsoever, to thrust open any door whatever, to kill whomever they pleased, to choose the woman who attracted them, to take her without having to beg for her favours, to slay her with the advent of post-coital disgust. To drink, to rest, to start again. Absolute freedom, yes, superhuman powers. For the duration of a night they could feel themselves to be the equals of the gods. And there was this poor Cuban lecturing them about respect for revolutionary order and the need to become industrious socialists . . .

Deep down inside himself Elias sensed the presence of someone (someone ignoble!) who was ready to prove the soldiers right. Not that he would have wished to approve of their type of happiness. But here in the depths of a jungle where these young men had daily brushes with death, this banquet of flesh and violence had a sombre justification. A simple sub-machine gun made all-powerful beings of these peasants, offering in a few nights of orgy all that an ordinary man can scarcely hope for from a whole lifetime.

It was terrifying to tell himself that these soldiers might be right. And to feel he was one of them.

Elias walked a little way through the throng of bodies numbed with drunkenness and drugs, and suddenly remembered that it was his birthday. He was sixteen . . . He had the impression of a long vista opening up before him, a vortex of encounters, faces, new things to explore, to taste, to conquer. All the infinite richness of human life . . .

A shadow stirred in the darkness, he stepped back, peered intently. A drunken woman, almost naked, was extricating herself from the embrace of a sleeping man. She was seated now, her eyes glinting in the moonlight, her body rendered blue by its phosphorescence. Her mouth was gasping for air, her broad thighs formed a dark, hollow triangle . . . Elias told himself it would be so easy to copy the soldiers, to crouch down, to thrust the woman onto her back, to plunge into that dark triangle.

The infinite richness of life . . . As he moved away he reflected that this one night alone concentrated within it all that man desires, fears, hopes for, detests. There was the victors' jubilation and the despair of the vanquished. Ernesto's vibrant homily and the soldiers' abusive mockery. Dead flesh and bodies stirred with pleasure. The abundance of food and the famine that from tomorrow would torment the survivors of this ravaged village. There was the almost godlike freedom the soldiers took upon themselves in killing, raping and torturing, and the subjection of those who, reduced to a mass of pain, were the victims of this freedom. There was the sky above and, doubtless, a god to whom so many suppliant voices were raised, but who remained silent, did not intervene, allowed a child to turn itself into a ball of flesh, wedged between the legs of a little table.

The whole world was condensed into that night. And yet something was missing. The essential thing was missing. Elias felt this lack like a gentle pressure on his eyelids: those evenings long ago, the threshold of their house in Dondo and his mother still, silent, as he hid his face in the crook of her arm. Life throbbed softly beneath the smooth curve of that arm . . . The essential thing was this love, and that was what was missing from this world. Each of the women who had just been raped and killed had carried this universe of tenderness and peace in the crook of her arm. Each of the men killing or being killed had been that child pressing his face against his mother's arm. All that was needed was to say this, to get other people to understand this.

It was thanks to this train of thought, he later realized, that he did not go out of his mind during that murderous night.

* * *

The following morning the fighter in his new khaki uniform who had demanded payment of his wages from Ernesto a week earlier, reported to the 'command post'. 'I've had several of the arsonists shot, *Commandante*,' he announced. 'Now's the time to talk to the troops. Raise their political consciousness . . . Sober them up, while you're at it . . .' He said it with the same mocking disdain, the assurance of one who knows himself to be master of the situation. 'I've witnessed the birth of a warlord,' Elias would one day reflect, when that race of killers was taking possession of the contṇent.

Ernesto left Africa a week after that night of fire. Elias saw him vigorously cramming a bundle of notebooks tied with string into his pack. The reason for his departure was just and noble, like everything the Cuban proclaimed in his speeches: he was going to carry the torch of the revolutionary struggle elsewhere, to seek the support of liberation movements in fraternal nations. He said this in grave, inspired tones and as they heard him they savoured the slightly faded piquancy of that verbal drug so intoxicating to men's souls.

Jacqueline followed him almost immediately but hers was a noisy, resentful flight. In the flood of reproaches she poured forth right up to the last minute, what stayed in Elias's mind was this regret which, for him, best defined the true nature of white people: 'It could have been a fascinating experiment!' Jacqueline exclaimed. 'I could have launched a veritable cultural revolution, starting with film, the art form most accessible to the people . . .' The whole of the West was there, thought Elias. The arrogant desire to transform other people's lives into an 'experiment', into a testing ground for their own ideas. And then, if this human material resists, to abandon it, to move on in search of a more malleable one.

Most of all, he grasped the very great difference between two types of revolutionary: those who could pack their bags, depart, settle somewhere else, and those who did not have this choice. Elias's father remained.

From then on their struggle was harsher, more primitive and also more authentic. The day-to-day battle for survival of a handful of men. Elias noted that the resistance of the defeated expressed the essence of war better than grand strategies and glorious victories. The fury of their fighting no longer had any goal beyond that moment at nightfall, after the final shots, when they found themselves still alive, another day of reprieve, when the glances they exchanged were silently eloquent of their poignant closeness as human beings.

Previously Ernesto's speeches had given a semblance of logic to the endless treks through the forest, the gun battles, the deaths of young men who had lived so little. Such deaths did not seem pointless now, but rather directed towards a different destination, like the light of that constellation reflected in the eyes of the wounded soldier Elias gave a drink to. His lips were still moving under the trickle of water, the iris in his eyes caught the glittering of the night, then suddenly everything froze, the mouth, the eyelashes . . . As he closed the eyelids it seemed to Elias as if these eyes still perceived the dark abyss of the sky more broadly than ever. This was the very first man he had kept company with as he died.

Defeat taught him a lot. One day, hidden in a thicket, he saw soldiers finishing off wounded men watched by their commander, that soldier in a new uniform, the man he had thought capable of changing sides for more pay. He had done so and was now hunting down the diminishing number of rebels led by Elias's father.

The rout transformed his father as well. He was no longer the operatic revolutionary in his fancy uniform that made him look like a Portuguese officer. No, like the fighters he was trying to extricate from the encirclement, his father was russet with dust, bearded, his eyes reddened from lack of sleep, from the sun and from stress. He had a limp in his left leg, hit by shrapnel, and the calf was swathed in dirty bandages.

Elias realized that before coming to the Congo this was how he had pictured his father.

One evening, passing through a village, Elias caught sight of two women, one young, the other older, half-heartedly arguing as they prepared a meal. He stopped, struck by the similarity: this was an exact replica of what he had seen that very first day, on his arrival at the rebel camp . . . The same actions, the same voices, the same serenity. All of it perfectly indifferent to Ernesto's speeches, to the violence of the fighting, to the promises of a better world. These women's happiness had nothing exalted about it and yet happiness it was: the golden haze of the sunset on the road, the cries of the children among the huts, the smell of food and the cool breeze already filtering up from the river, the gentle lapping of the water beneath an oar . . . In a train of thought he did not succeed in following through to the end, he told himself that this happiness presented a greater threat to Ernesto's revolution than any class enemy.

* * *

Finally there came a moment when the very thing that gave strength to their band on the run, the tie, the blood-soaked bond, became its principal flaw: together, they were easily identifiable, they needed to separate and, one by one, 'blend in with the populace'. Elias remembered Ernesto instructing the soldiers in this technique.

He had already read, and would later read again, scenes in books of farewells between comrades in arms. These featured ringing turns of phrase, solemn oaths, tears choked back and, if a loving woman was involved, long embraces interrupted only by the revving of engines. Their own parting had nothing melodramatic about it. They counted up and shared out the remaining ammunition, then did the same with the food and the scant medical supplies. His father, followed by several men, took up position between two hills to allow the others to move away safely, to escape the commando units which had tight surveillance of the area. Elias did not even really have time to talk to him and it was only the next day that the meaning of their separation became clear: impossible now to ask all the questions that had been slowly accumulating within him since his arrival in the Congo.

A week later this impossibility of talking felt like a suffocation. For he saw his father again.

Mingling with a group of peasants in flight from the fighting, Elias was standing on the high bank of a river and, like them, watching a boat as it travelled past. A man was rowing with all his strength to pull away from the shore where soldiers were directing almost continuous gunfire at him. The grimaces of the men shooting could be made out clearly down below as they aimed long bursts in the direction of the boat. The face of the man in flight was clearly visible too: his mouth urgently gasping for breath, a vagabond's beard, that roll of bandages on the left calf . . . His father. A man about to be killed at any moment . . .

To prevent this death he would have had to throw himself from the top of the bank, roll down the slope, rush at the soldiers and . . . And be killed by the first bullet. Elias remained motionless, hypnotized by the spurts from bullets hitting the water around the boat, as if in a random game.

The distance was already considerable, the shooting from the sub-machine guns lacked precision, the soldiers swore, got annoyed, their aim became even wilder. For a moment Elias believed, hoped with all his being, that his father was going to escape.

It was then that he saw the white man with a ginger moustache and red patches on his round face, smiling and dour at the same time. Of average height, stocky, his bow legs in khaki shorts, he had the air of a professional irritated by the incompetence of amateurs. Unhurriedly, he set up the mount of his machine gun on the sand, cleared the sights, took a drag on his cigarette and laid the stub down on a rock. Aimed, fired . . . And smiled condescendingly at the soldiers as they applauded him. In the distance the fugitive, struck in the head and throat, threw up his arms, let go the oars, fell backwards. The boat continued in its course across the river, then began to drift. The ginger-haired man picked up his cigarette again, exhaled a slow curl of smoke.

When Elias had the strength to think, he told himself

that his father's death resembled the fall of a bird hit in mid flight. He did not know why but this image made his grief less appalling.

One of Ernesto's promises was kept. Travelling via clandestine networks, then via Algeria and East Germany, Elias managed to reach Cuba. It felt as if he were travelling through time, towards an encounter with a dream that had already been realized, one that in Africa was barely beginning to put out shoots, nourished by endless tides of blood.

Aftermath of a Dream

I

Cuba would teach him the use of weapons, the science of revolution, the flesh of woman. Then one evening, in 1967, on a beach bathed in the sunset's copper light, he learned that Ernesto had met his end.

So it was that this death remained forever associated in his memory with the vivid blood-red clouds, the sleepy swell of the waves and the tear-stained face of the young Cuban woman who broke the news to him. Hair stiff with salt, lips on which he silenced her somewhat over-artistic lamentation with a kiss: 'Che is dead! The Americans have killed him . . .' Ernesto's death mingled with the smooth warmth of the first body he had loved, now shaken with sobs.

Elias sensed the coquettish element in her grief. His girlfriend had met him to make love, to which she generally applied herself with fierce, healthy zest, wasting no time on emotional outpourings. The national hero's death brought a new savour of drama to their encounter. Thanks to these slightly forced tears, he grasped that it was possible for love to be no more than this: two bodies taking pleasure, parting, tangling with each other again . . . Sometimes, a few theatrical effects could add spice to this sweet physical fulfilment. Slivers of moonlight on the sea, tender little lies tickling an ear, the feeble death throes of a wave, the choking death throes of a guerilla in the Bolivian jungle . . .

He lay there beside the woman glowing with pleasure and was amazed as one of those thoughts struck him, simple enough to be almost banal in their aptness: 'So the revolution hasn't changed any of this!'

Three years later, during a mass meeting in Havana, the same idea about love and revolution occurred to him: just as crude a consideration and just as disconcertingly lucid. And yet he had meanwhile made good progress in the study of the armed struggle, of Marxist theory, and he thought he knew what women, with their beauty, their strength and their vulnerability, could give, and could not give, a man. But the question that had troubled him in the old days remained as clear and insoluble as ever: 'If the revolution doesn't change the way we love, what's the point of all this fighting?'

Motionless in the line-up of his comrades, young soldiers like himself, he was watching the vast open space crowded with the 'toiling masses', who were being warmed up by the speakers before Castro took the floor. Slogans rattled out on the wind with the slashing resonance of Spanish, the applause and shouting erupted in long, foaming waves. From his place behind the platform, Elias could see the speakers' backs and the reverse side of two enormous banners. The sunlight was so strong that the painted figures showed through and could be recognized. Marx and Engels to the right of the rostrum, Lenin and Castro to the left. He was not listening to the harangues but noting the bizarre features of the spectacle. Unusually, the four mentors of humanity were shown full length on the canvas of the banners; generally only their heads were portrayed. The reverse side of the canvas was punctuated with nails which held it to the framework of wooden struts. Curiously, the thought that one of the nails had been driven into Engels' chest and another had pierced Castro's beard rendered the speeches both ludicrous and ambiguous. *Libertad . . . Movimiento . . . Histórico . . . Poder Popular . . .* The faces in the crowd smiled foolishly, as if watching a film, while the backs of the banners revealed fabric frayed at the edges.

A woman with blonde hair mounted the platform and the impression of a staged performance increased. She spoke with a strong accent, gesticulating. Elias experienced the unease that is felt when a person dear to one makes a public appearance. Especially a woman recently held in one's arms, kissed, pleasured. An inane pride ('They're cheering a woman I've just slept with') and shame, as if the two of them had suddenly exposed themselves naked.

He had known Louise Rimens for several months. A Frenchwoman from a very wealthy family, who had broken with her background and 'married the revolution', as she put it. At first Elias perceived hers as a unique and exemplary life story, before learning that the agitation among the young in '68 had spawned hordes of apprentice rebels who were now at large in those countries where they could still fan the embers and lead lives capable of shocking their bourgeois parents. Everything Louise did in Cuba was, consciously or not, directed at an imaginary audience back in France.

Now she was calling for the flame of revolt to be

spread to other continents. ('For there are no flame-proof countries anywhere in the world!' Where on earth did she learn these expressions?) Her voice faltered when she mentioned Ernesto Guevara. And within the enclosed space behind the lectern her feet were arranged in a ridiculous and touching manner: her heels splayed out and her big toes pressed together. Her body was robust but not graceful. The plumpness of a young woman from a good family (plentiful food, riding, holidays in a vast country house), a young woman eager at all costs to take advantage of the benefits of her bourgeois youth in adventures at the other end of the world, among starving populations, upheavals and struggles.

It all seemed so clear to Elias now! A little girl of twenty-five, a spoiled child, busy crafting a life story for herself. Manipulating the modelling clay that had come to hand: this Cuba in ferment, this Havana crowd drinking in her words like those of a prophet (so she believed), the enthusiastic articles she sent to a Paris newspaper and 'Che', an icon, immortal, because he had died at the right moment . . . 'And myself too, an exotic lover, the embodiment of "negritude", a perfect feature of the whole scenario . . .'

He had never sensed this so plainly before. So all it took was to be located behind the platform, to see the backs of the banners and the nails driven through the bodies of the revolutionaries ('There, squarely in Fidel's crotch,' he noted, repressing an untoward smile), to notice Louise's feet. Her French accent, after the harshness of the Spanish, made one think of a cabaret singer's rhyming lyrics.

'It's play-acting,' he reflected, recalling how that young

Cuban woman had sobbed three years earlier, as she gave him the news of Ernesto's death. 'Yes, it's still the same play-acting, except that I now have the enviable role of male juvenile lead in it . . .'

Then it was as if a flood of fresh and disconcerting perceptions suddenly struck him. He reflected that the persona of the black lover, with a legendary warrior's aura, would certainly turn out to be the heartthrob role white women would adore casting him in. And that a male model like this would attract European women of a very specific type: disaffected young middle-class women with a mania for heroic exoticism. Rather plain women who would instinctively home in on that sought after male, the black man they believe eager to possess a white woman . . . He suddenly realized that Louise was very similar to his father's companion, the Belgian woman who had abandoned, or rather betrayed, them in the Congo. And that this Frenchwoman, too, was free to leave whenever the fancy took her. And that he, the black lover, would disappear from her life as soon as the curtain fell. And that, in truth, she despised this crowd of Cubans, because instead of flying to Che's rescue, they got married, grilled fish in stinking oil, dreamed of buying cars . . . And that she was consuming the revolution just as, in Europe, she would have consumed food and clothes, and that, for her, he himself, his black skin, his body, his genitals, were also consumer goods . . .

Castro's voice broke in on this tumble of bitter thoughts. The orator was speaking with somewhat mournful sincerity, with vehement and at the same time melancholy conviction. 'The conviction of someone who no longer believes, but who wants at all costs to be believed,' Elias would reflect years later.

As for himself, he wanted to hold on to his faith at all costs. That ancient, still childlike hope of seeing a world where it would be impossible to leave a woman to die with a broken collarbone, or to gun a man down, almost absent-mindedly, between two drags on a cigarette.

Towards the end of the speech he felt a light tickle on his back. A whisper brushed his ear: 'I'll be waiting for you at my place. Try to get away.' Louise had managed to insinuate herself in between the ranks of the soldiers. Without seeing her, Elias was aware of that great child's gleeful excitement, her passion for clandestine adventures and secret rendezvous. He looked at his watch (Castro had been speaking for more than two hours) and noted that, in exalting the society of the future, at no point had the orator referred to the love between two human beings.

That evening at Louise's place he was back again in the masquerade of conspiracy, the falseness of which he now perceived so clearly. A warrior under threat (himself) meets up with his *pasionaria* (her) in the middle of a hostile country, in an unknown city. That must have been how Louise mythologized their nights together. She opened the door and flung her arms about him as if they had not seen one another for months, as if he had had to cross minefields and pass through bursts of gunfire. He wanted to tell her he had just strolled whistling out of the barracks and the greatest danger he had been in during the past few months had been that of falling overboard from an inflatable craft during landing exercises. And in that neighbourhood everyone was quietly getting on with frying fish . . . She knew all this but simply did not want to destroy the illusion.

Wholly immersed in her role as a rebel on the run, she gave herself, enjoyed more intense pleasure than ever, thanks to this game, and grew bolder. It was the actress in her that drew him down onto the floor of her room, let herself be ravished there on the ground, amid cigarette ends and the scattered drafts of her articles. It was the make-believe revolutionary who clawed at his belly, moaning and biting her lip, flung herself onto her back in the posture of one crucified, feigning now the self-abasement of a submissive lover, now the mechanical stubbornness of a female slow to be satisfied.

Until very recently these carnal games had flattered him. What he had beheld in the woman's distraught look, her wild eye, was the reflection of his own virility, the black gleam of his sweating skin, the mark of his new status: he, the African, was servicing a well-known journalist, a white woman who was on close terms with the Cuban leaders and Castro himself.

That evening these masks struck him as a hollow sham. But, to crown it all, he realized that it had been a hollow sham from the start.

Louise stirred on the floor, stood up, still drugged with pleasure, and staggered towards the bed. Comically, a page of typescript clung to her right buttock. Elias stretched out his arm, detached the page and by the light of a bulb suspended over a typewriter, glimpsed this sentence: 'Every revolution is at risk from two dangers:

the gangrene of bureaucracy in its leaders and the recurrence of petty bourgeois instincts in the workers . . .' The sickly sweet smell of maize as well as that of fried fish, pungent and oily, floated in through the bedroom window. 'The alimentary instincts of the petty bourgeoisie . . .' thought Elias, smiling in the dim light.

And she did indeed start to talk about how the revolutionaries of twelve years ago were being visibly tempted today by the siren voices of Florida. 'A lack of political consciousness . . . The American influence . . . The lure of the dollar . . .' The sense of her words should have called for brisk, severe tones. But the woman was torpid after her physical exertions and nestled up to the man with the abandon of any romantic young mistress.

He already knew how the evening would go. The impassioned revolutionary, having become a languid lover, was going to mutate into a good western tourist, with an expert knowledge of picturesque Havana. She would take him out to their 'favourite' restaurant, order their 'favourite' dishes, greet their 'favourite' chef . . . She would have done the same in Provence, in China, in Senegal.

A Frenchwoman who knows how to explore the local attractions. 'Revolutionary tourism . . .' he thought, surprised, himself, by the aptness of the phrase.

The dinner began as expected. Except that this time Elias was waiting for an opportunity at last to tell the truth. And this anticipation made the setting seem increasingly artificial: the sea breeze with its 'faint whiff of iodine', as Louise always remarked, the sugary strumming of a guitar, the momentary fire of the rum.

He did not know where to start. Perhaps with the falsity of the parts they were playing. She a tourist in the zoo of revolution. He the symbolic negro breaking the shackles of slavery. Or should he talk to her about the 'Che' he had known? Describe him as he had appeared in Africa, a real man still, with all his fears and weaknesses? Yes, tell her the story of just that night amid drunken soldiers laying siege to their 'command post'. Tell her how Che and the Belgian woman had fled, frightened by the devastating chaos that prevailed in the bestiary of African revolutions. Say to her: 'You'll cut and run, too, when you've had enough. And I'll end up in your notebook, among the other trophies, a brief episode in your tourist expedition. Yes, my negro's head hung on the wall in your drawing room, between a Parisian anarchist and a Cuban *barbudo* . . .'

The image of it struck him as comic, he smiled and noticed then that they had both been silent for a moment, casting wary glances at one another and knocking back their rum with equal wariness. Louise had a harsh, scornful grimace. He had a fervent desire to reclaim from this woman all that she had had from him: their nights together, his African body that she had added to her collection . . . He again pictured his head as a hunting trophy and realized the extent to which all this was unimportant: his inveighing against the Westerners' revolutionary safaris, his bouts with Louise in theatrical secrecy, the pleasure this big child had taken, having indeed come here in the hope of indulging in sex, spiced with battles and impassioned speeches . . . He felt so little involved in this vortex of words and deeds, of the ebb and flow of passions. The essential thing was still that child hiding a wounded bird inside his shirt, a child who found the world's perfection in the fold of his mother's arm . . . If only he could tell her about that!

He looked up and suddenly became aware that Louise was talking, or rather muttering, in inebriated but lucid tones, and that she was saying precisely what he had been preparing to declare. 'Che's soon going to turn into a mascot, a caricature, a label . . . Do you think I don't understand that? But people need something to believe in . . . Otherwise it's, you know, Orwell, Kafka . . . Besides, who could replace him? Fidel? A man who goes on jabbering for hours in his sleep? Our European revolutionaries? They never venture further afield than the last stop on the metro . . . Go ahead. Tell me, if that's what you think. Tell me I'm just like them. A spoiled young bourgeoise. Cruising the world to get screwed by guys with ebony skins hung like stallions . . . You owe it to yourself to think that, don't you? And what's more I'm this slapper who's trying to get herself a CV to match the bare-breasted girl on the barricades.'

Her tone began to waver, now aggressive, abusive of herself and others, now helpless and tender. She talked about a blind dog she had in Paris, confessed to having betrayed it by going away to make 'her little revolution'. Then, without transition, declared: 'But did you know the Cuban leaders are hiding the journal Che kept in the Congo? His notebooks. Not the notes that have been published . . . I've tried everything to get my hands on them. It's a State Secret, you know! But I did find out from a Frenchman with contacts close to Castro that there was a fragment headed: *When Revolutions Die*. It sounds as if he was talking about the Cuban revolution. All those leaders. They've started to stink of rancid archives . . .'

She was almost shouting. Then, when Elias managed to take her out, to escort her home, she wept and babbled with the pitiful and touching incoherence of a drunken woman, whom one would like simultaneously to fold in one's arms and to slap. She said her father had 'the look of someone who'd been in the O.A.S.'; that her mother's life was 'as lively as a barnacle'; that it was better 'to be wrong with Sartre'; that her grandmother recited poetry to her flowers and was the only honest person in their family; that power grew 'out of the barrel of a gun'. Finally, in a quavering avowal, she denounced the perfidy of a certain Jean-Yves, who had dumped her for a 'fat German cow, a friend of Andreas Baader. But I'll show him, that bastard. I'll show him,' she gulped. 'Here in Cuba, I'm going to . . .'

Her voice drowned in a sob, Elias drew her to him, cradled the head racked with shudders against his shoulder. As the veil of sleep descended, Louise was still murmuring, calling someone. Her blind dog left in Paris, Elias guessed.

That night was the only one where they felt truly close, liberated from the postures they had imposed on themselves. And for the first time Elias became aware of the paths that led human beings through revolutions and wars, through life. He grasped that within the most stubborn commitment to the most sublime cause could lie hidden the desire to punish a man who went off with a rival, the memory of an old woman who recited poetry to her window boxes and pity for a dog.

He slept little, listened to the plaintive breathing of

the woman squeezed tight against his arm, studied the photos that seemed to meet his gaze in the phosphorescent glow of the nightlight. Hemingway as a boxer in a ring, the charmer's smile directed at the photographer. Castro at the centre of a crowd, in which, if you looked carefully, according to Louise, you could make her out. Malraux elegant and ambiguous, like a croupier in a casino. And finally Che, with eyes ablaze and wild hair. And lower down a caricature: de Gaulle transformed into Hitler, with the SS insignia on his shoulder . . . 'They must all have had a blind dog in their lives . . .' thought Elias.

During the days that followed Louise avoided him and when they ran into one another more or less by chance, he perceived that she had fully regained her self-possession. 'Wow! That was a hell of a binge!' she exclaimed, very much at her ease. 'I must have spouted a lot of crap at you . . .'

She left Cuba a month later, without letting him know in advance. A note reached him the day after her departure. 'I was frankly disappointed with the way the revolution was going,' she wrote. 'And I never hid that from you.' She also mentioned that the Paris newspaper she had been working for was offering her a job . . .

Two years later, by then in Moscow, Elias would learn of the publication of Louise Rimens' book. The title would be a surprise and yet no surprise to him: *When Revolutions Die . . .*

*   *   *

During the rest of his time in Havana he often tried to find a logic in this frenzy of human beings committed to what seemed like a monolith: History, the Revolution. A young woman taking her revenge on a faithless lover by falling in love with Che, wishing to set the whole world on fire and recalling her grandmother's house with poignant nostalgia. A woman ready to sacrifice millions of human lives on the altar of an Idea but who wept when she thought about her blind dog . . .

'The contradictions of existence,' he thought with a smile, recalling his studies in philosophy. Or perhaps quite simply a lack of professionalism on the part of these amateur revolutionaries?

Then he thought about the USSR, the country his father's friends used to give as an example of 'a society of the future conceived along purely scientific lines'. In Cuba the Russians seemed to be accomplishing a task that was almost routine for them, that of constructing a world others could only dream about. On the facade of one of the factories they were erecting he had one day read: 'Our tasks are resolved, our goals are clear! To work, comrades!' In this slogan, simplistic though it was, could be read an unshakeable certainty that was lacking in the dilettantes of the liberation struggles.

On the plane to Moscow he was thinking about the title of 'professional revolutionary' that his father used to lay claim to, as did Ernesto. And which Lenin bore. Then he came to grasp the difference between amateurism and professionalism in revolution. The professional never asks himself the question 'What's the point?', only 'By what means?' since he has no life apart from the dream whose realization he is irresistibly and patiently engaged in.

Seventeen years later, at the end of the '80s, we met in Florida at Fort Lauderdale. It occurred to us that those Cubans who were bailing out from their island in distress might well be landing not very far from these shores. Still more obvious than Cuba's pitching and tossing, however, was the impending shipwreck of that great ocean liner, the USSR. I had never questioned Elias so frankly about the blindness of those who, like him, sacrificed their lives to a cause. 'I've often heard intellectuals declaring that thanks to such and such an event the scales had fallen from their eyes,' he replied. 'That they had seen nothing blameworthy in a regime until all at once what had seemed magnificent the day before became contemptible. Yes, the USSR, Mao and now Castro. Almost twenty years ago I knew a woman, a French journalist working in Havana. She wrote a book to explain how she had suddenly realized that the Cuban revolution was nothing but an appalling dictatorship. Well, you know, I never thought our struggle was perfect or that the people engaged in it were saints. But I've always believed in the need for a different world. And I still believe in it.'

This answer must then have struck him as too solemn and abstract, too bound up with the ideas of his youth. He inclined his head slightly: 'You see that fellow over there, yes, the one in shorts. With a spotted shirt. The steak he's eating weighs at least a pound. His country, America, defends this man's right to eat that amount of meat with all its might. And especially his right not to give a damn that on the opposite shore of the Atlantic children with amputated arms are chewing on bark to assuage their hunger before they die. And yet the two shores are one and the same world. You just need to take the long view, to stand up on tiptoe, like this, to see it.'

He did just this, stood up in the middle of the restaurant terrace where we were sitting.

This is one of the clearest images I shall retain of him: a man upright, straight as a blade, towering above the crowd of diners.

II

What was hardest, as always, was steeling oneself to kill the children. The offspring of a tyrant, of course, the future elite of an oppressive regime. But, once the door to their bedroom was smashed in, Elias turned away, in spite of himself, to avoid the gaze of the little boy trying to hide behind the curtain, the little girl clutching a big doll in a foam of lace . . .

The airport had been taken an hour earlier, just after the crushing of the state guard and the occupation of the armoury. Commandos held the railway station, the principal roads, the main banks. The assault was delayed by unexpected resistance around the radio station. But the presidential palace was already reverberating with gunfire. The orders were clear: to liquidate the head of state as well as all the members of his family, without exception. Left alive, one of the sons could have become the rallying point for counter-revolution.

Leading his unit, Elias reached the first floor, passed through the continuous fire of the bodyguard, assisted the engineer to blow in the door to the private apartments. The assault troops machine-gunned every nook and cranny, covering one another on the staircases and at the corners of corridors, threw grenades. And then came that children's bedroom, the impulse to shoot without killing, keeping one's eyes shut, or even to be

killed before being able to kill . . . They informed him
that the secret police defending the radio station had
been dislodged. He had to leap into a jeep, force a way
through the bursts of fire and, once quickly installed in
front of a microphone, read out the *Declaration by the
Provisional Popular Government* he had drafted the day
before: 'Comrades! The heroic struggle of the Army of
National Liberation has put an end to the bloody and
corrupt dictatorship of Marshal X. Power is in the hands
of the people, represented by the patriotic forces of the
ANL and the Socialist Party of Progress . . .'

Highly professional work, from the first shots fired
in the morning right through to this broadcast, in a
studio still smelling of the acrid reek of gunpowder and
the sweat of breathless men. Elias read in grave tones,
his eyes sometimes straying from the typewritten lines,
he knew the text by heart. At one moment, looking up,
he noticed a large jar half filled with a cloudy liquid at
the other end of the desk. He suppressed a smile: here
in the heart of a third-world country, right in the middle
of a revolution, these marinaded tomatoes, with their
label in Russian . . .

Each time, in this final phase of seizing power, this
jar would make its appearance: someone had left it
behind in the building where the Soviet instructors
taught the art of overthrowing dictatorships. And each
time, moved at having addressed the population of a
whole country, Elias would forget to throw away these
tomatoes, steeped in their murky marinade.

He had already taken part in a dozen revolutionary
training exercises in that military camp close to Moscow.

The scenario would vary: the enemy forces would become better armed and differently deployed, the pitfalls would multiply, the 'population' (played by soldiers in civilian clothes) was sometimes cooperative, sometimes hostile. The city itself, an artificial city, a replica of a typical urban layout, with its railway station, the residence of the head of state, the airport and the rest of the key locations, yes, even these prefabricated blocks, would be rearranged before the next revolution. This made the insurgents' action more complicated: the station was transformed into a barracks, the secret police head-quarters became the American Embassy, the approaches to the airport were now protected by minefields . . . Inside the presidential palace the allocation of rooms was not constant either. The tyrant's office could be recognized thanks to a large framed reproduction of *The Battle of Borodino*. And on the threshold of the children's room they put that great plastic doll wrapped in grubby tulle, with one arm missing.

In each exercise everything would change. Except for that jar of tomatoes in the studio at the national radio station. And also that unease when it came to firing at the phantom children. One day Elias caught himself imagining faces he had seen in Dondo, in Kivu, in Cuba . . .

A revolution, the instructors used to say, is not just a matter of explosives. It takes long and meticulous prepar-ation. Initially the 'popular masses' must be worked on in depth, creating both networks of fighting men and looser ones of 'fellow travellers' and 'sympathizers', essential to the success of the uprising. The overthrow of a dictatorship cannot be embarked on without first infiltrating the army and the police, winning the approval, or at least the neutrality, of the intellectuals and the media and sounding out the diplomatic terrain. But ultimately it is a question of having a nose for it: a people ready to support you, a regime ripe for collapse, these things can be smelled. 'But it still reeks of explosives . . .' thought Elias, sensing the deeply held conviction of his masters in revolution.

And when your nose failed you the specialists were there to guide you. These instructors had taken part in the overthrow of plenty of regimes, their experience was undeniable. 'Professional revolutionaries,' Elias reminded himself. On one occasion, they would recount, the kin of the former dictator had been spared; the result: civil war broke out again for another two years. In a coup d'état in Central America a banker who should have been subjected to 'specific means of pressure' (in plain language, torture or watching the simulated killing of his family) had simply been imprisoned and, after a successful escape, had set about financing a counter-revolution, thanks to his foreign bank accounts (which he would certainly have surrendered under torture). In South-East Asia, negligence over the execution of a British journalist: instead of using a sub-machine gun taken from the enemy, the soldiers had given themselves away by using their own service weapons . . .

At the end of all these sessions on insurrection techniques, so ingenious and ruthless were the tricks designed to outwit one's fellow human beings that Elias found himself asking: 'What's the point?' In the mouths of the instructors these tactics for fighting and subversion became art for art's sake, glorious goals in their own right, which eclipsed the goal of the revolution itself. They would spend their whole lives, Elias told himself, perfecting their methods, like chess players hypnotized by the marquetry of their own chessboards. 'What's the point?' . . . He hurriedly silenced this question, unworthy of a professional.

His study of Marx, which he returned to at Patrice Lumumba University, helped him to forget this dilettante questioning for a time. Despite the dogmatic solemnity with which the doctrine was taught, for him it still held the savour of that first intellectual revelation, his gropings under the direction of Carvalho, the vet in Dondo. He absorbed and expounded for the examiners the dialectical thickets of *Das Kapital*, but what remained in his memory was the somewhat crude clarity of Carvalho's observations: 'The world is governed by human beings' desire to dominate their fellows. Man's exploitation of man. Marx was right! Look at the Portuguese and the colonized peoples. And the rich Portuguese and the poor Portuguese . . . No truce can ever be possible.' And he would go on to talk about the class struggle.

And this struggle, Elias now recalled, meant the impaled heads of Angolans displayed alongside the fields, like scarecrows . . . 'For a capitalist,' Carvalho explained, 'everything becomes a commodity, everything!' In *Das Kapital* Elias discovered the secret of this world up for sale. But one step ahead of his comprehension, his memory turned a spotlight on a room painted yellow, where an ugly little soldier, entangled in his lowered trousers, hopped up and down in front of a naked, unbearably beautiful black woman. 'Commodity – money – commodity,' was Marx's formula. This naked body transformed into a commodity produced money which, in its turn, became a commodity again: bread brought by the woman to her child, Elias.

Later on, during his travels in Europe, he would often hear intellectuals referring, with a little sneer of contempt, to 'the Marxist Bible'. Then he would remember his studies in Moscow, aware that his fellow students could all have been accused of taking their expositions of Marx too lightly. Except that for them this much-derided Bible carried with it the crushing weight of the dead, the grief of years of battles and humiliations.

One day doubt assailed him in the most unexpected way. He had just been masterminding the seizure of the airport in that mock-up of a city in which so many successful revolutions took place. The coach taking them back to Moscow broke down and his companions in arms, both the 'revolutionaries' and the 'henchmen of the dictatorship' set off towards a suburban railway station. He decided to return on foot, intoxicated by the softness of the snow silvering the empty fields and low roofs of a few mournful houses. The first snow since his arrival in Moscow. The first snow of his life. He had imagined a stinging, numbing cold. Now, feeling these large, almost lukewarm, snowflakes brushing against his face, he broke into a joyful smile.

On what was still partly a country road he noticed a very old woman walking so slowly that it looked as if every step she took was set down with great care upon the delicate white embroidery. In a string shopping bag she carried several packets parcelled up in coarse grey paper and a loaf wrapped in newspaper. As she made her way round a puddle of water, she steadied herself on the branch of an apple tree that leaned out over the road. Elias suddenly had a profound perception of the moment linking that aged hand with the gnarled bark. The woman stopped, raised her face towards the whirling snow. He believed she was smiling faintly.

He often thought of that woman again. In a world where the poor, fated to be unhappy, were engaged in their class struggle against the rich, who were inevitably brimming over with happiness, it was difficult to find a place for this elderly passer-by on the day of the first snow. Was she poor? Certainly. Markedly more deprived, indeed, than the 'popular masses' in capitalist societies, battling against the bourgeoisie. But was she unhappy? Elias already knew enough about life in Russia to know the extent to which these unremarked lives could be mysteriously replete with meaning. Besides, would she have been happier if her bag had been bulging with food? If, instead of having passed through wars, purges, famines, she had led a calm and fortunate existence somewhere in the West?

These questions seemed to him childish and even foolish, and yet they disturbed the rigour of the theories he was learning at the university. An old woman, walking slowly on the day of the first snow, leans on a branch, looks up towards the flurry of snowflakes . . . Impossible to find a place for this human being in the propaganda trio one saw everywhere on the facades of buildings in Moscow: a worker with muscular arms, a *kolkhoznik* laden with sheaves of wheat, a bespectacled intellectual with his scientific instruments. These three classes symbolized the present and the future of the country. The old woman was not of their time. 'Like so many others in this country . . .' thought Elias. A whole stratum of life was excluded from the philosophers' fine systems.

From that day onwards he travelled a lot on foot, in the hope of discovering behind the facades a world peopled by these unclassifiable human beings who challenged Marx.

One of these strolls on the outskirts of Moscow nearly cost him dear. He was walking that evening through the heart of an outer suburb where dreary prefabricated dwellings stood cheek by jowl with old wooden houses and structures from the post-war years, those long, single-storey erections where in Stalin's day they deposited the workmen recruited for the reconstruction of Moscow. Occasionally a dark brick wall would rear up, concealing the blackened buildings of a factory. Whether alone or in groups, people walked quickly and in silence, as if to get away from the area.

Elias was familiar with the different reactions his face provoked. Often a discreet but hostile curiosity, a quick, astonished glance: 'What's that negro doing here?' Some people, especially the young, had no hesitation in saying it. Occasionally, on the other hand, a broad smile which ought to signify tolerance and hospitality, the ploy he feared the most. Rarely simple indifference, which he preferred. But that evening the snow was falling copiously and under the cover of this moving curtain his progress attracted very little attention. His pace was matched by an apparently very simple train of thought. 'What I can see is the outcome, admittedly only provisional, of three revolutions, several wars, and the work of two hundred million men and women who for over half a century have been building a new world, in accordance with a grand plan, the dream of humanity . . .'

He did not notice at what moment the lane he was following began to run alongside a snow-covered railway track, then dipped beneath the crumbling roof of a kind of train depot. He stopped, attempted to retrace his footsteps and realized that it was already too late to escape.

'Bugger me! They forgot to shut the cages at the zoo. Look, there's a monkey! Any minute now we'll see a giraffe!' Elias met the eye of the man who had just spoken. Then all the men, seated in a semi-circle, howled with laughter. They were sitting round a metal stove, whose open top belched out flames and acrid, purplish smoke. One of them withdrew a slender iron spike from the fire and plunged it into a bucket. The hissing of the steam mingled with the last of the guffaws. 'So what's your game, sunshine? You climb down out of your tree. You learn to walk. And, fuck me, on your first time out you come round to ours. Well, thanks a lot, you stupid sod! You've made our day . . .' The men laughed again, the one who had put the spike in the water did an imitation of a monkey jumping out of a tree, starting to hobble along on three legs and scratching the back of his neck with his fourth. Elias tried to back away but, looking round, he saw one of them behind him holding a strip of heated metal, clasped between leather mittens, with a glowing tip that appeared transparent. No threatening gestures, just scorn, almost casual.

This was not one of those little gangs of youths Elias had so far contrived to avoid. These were older men, he noted, caught off guard themselves by his appearance and seeking to divert attention from whatever they were up to through mockery. 'You can piss off now, Mr Ape. And we'll have your *shapka*. You won't need that in Africa. Go on. Fuck off! Get a move on! The zoo shuts in an hour . . .' A hand reached out towards his head. Elias pushed it away and at once a rapid blow from an iron rod knocked off his *shapka*. There was a perceptible smell of burning. He spun round and saw a wisp of smoke rising from the bottom of his coat.

'Go on, piss off! Don't you understand human language? Or do you want to be incinerated?' A white hot spike began waving about in front of his face. 'I need my *shapka* . . . It's snowing . . . And as for language, you're talking like those bastard slave drivers who . . .' Several men got up. 'Right, so you don't want to piss off on two legs like everyone else. Fair enough. You can go home on all fours like an ape . . .'

He was able to parry the first blows but suddenly felt a sharp burning on the back of his neck, could not repress a cry of pain, was thrown to the ground, dragged outside. A heavy boot kicked him in the head, his vision clouded over. He came to very quickly, tried to pick himself up, but was thrust back into a snowdrift. His cheek was pressing against the snow and this cold seemed salutary to him. With one hand he picked up a handful of ice, clamped it against his burning neck.

A kind of indifference overcame him. The physical pain was nothing beside the abyss that had just opened up within him. 'After three revolutions, several wars, over half a century of striving . . . The dream of humanity . . .' a faint echo reverberated in his head.

Even the words now ringing out above his body in the darkness seemed of no interest to him at first. And if they finally intrigued him it was because he could hardly understand a thing. And yet it was Russian. Not the foul-mouthed Russian often spoken in the streets of Moscow, whose smutty coarseness was familiar to him. No, a language whose rhythms he could make out very well, but whose words were quite unknown. Then he turned his head, trying to see whoever it was uttering these brief delphic sentences.

To the left of his face he saw a woman's shoes, of a heavy and ugly design, their leather all worn. Then coarse cotton stockings and the side of a dark coat made of rough woollen cloth. He pictured an elderly woman, the voice matched these clothes and that age, a dull, rather harsh voice. 'The old woman I saw on the day of the first snow . . .' he suddenly thought and, strangely, this hare-brained notion reassured him.

He heard the crunch of the snow beneath retreating footfalls, then felt a hand touching his head, his cheek. 'You can get up now. They've gone . . .'

He sat up and then, gritting his teeth to suppress a groan, rose to his feet. And remained on the spot for a long while, teetering slightly, not collapsing, thanks to the gaze that rested on him and sustained him. At that moment neither the woman's beauty nor her youth struck him. No word of gratitude formed in his head. There was this silence, the swirling of snow and a face that seemed to have been traced in the darkness by the incessant fluttering of the crystalline flakes.

He would later come to grasp that this was a beauty of an unusually high order. Others would speak of it to him, sometimes enviously, sometimes with regret: a gift from heaven too rich for a young woman from the provinces. And he would feel incapable of explaining that for him what was beautiful, too, was the touching ugliness of the battered shoes she wore that evening, and the muted music of their footfalls on a snow-covered road, and the resinous smell of the railway in the icy air . . .

Throughout his life he would have the impression that he could recall every minute ever spent with her, every twist and turn of the streets they followed together, every fleeting cloud shape above their heads. And yet in the moments closest to death, and therefore the most real, this would be the instant that came back to him, with the patient sorrow of his love: the sharp fragrance of snow, the stillness of a particular dusk and those eyes that had kept him upright.

'I thought I'd forgotten it, that language. And then when I heard those idiots the words came back to me. In an instant. That's all there was in our village: prisoners who'd been in the camps. They all dreamed of going off to a big city but they could never manage to get away. Those frozen lands held them captive. The truth is they were scared of not being able to get back into normal life. For a start there was this lingo they spoke in the camps . . . So they stayed. Even one of my family . . .' Her voice broke off, she murmured with a clumsy change of intonation: 'I'm Anna . . .'

Elias introduced himself. This only added to the feeling of unreality. They were walking along beneath great cascades of falling snow, as if in the middle of a flapping sail. He had tied the scarf the young woman had lent him over his head. He let himself be guided, in the insane hope that in the end all that had happened would be miraculously made good. Those men for whom he was nothing but a monkey, his *shapka* thrown in the fire, their hatred. In a country that promised a world without hatred . . .

'And these prisoners were common criminals, were they?' he asked. His voice betrayed his eager hope of a way out.

'No. The common criminals managed pretty well at

making a fresh start. At least a thief knows why he's
been put in prison. These were politicals. Absurd cases.
A *kolkhoznik* had dumped some manure on his vegetable
patch. It was just his luck that it was Stalin's birthday,
and they'd hung up his portrait on the house across the
road. The fellow got twenty years. After serving his
sentence he was still baffled by how a whole life can be
buried under a pile of dung. Well, in fact, it was me that
couldn't understand how he could go on living. Because
he did live. He went hunting now and then in the *taiga*.
Even made a collection of dried plants . . . Or there was
that student who, when he was taking notes, wrote down
"SOSialism". For a joke. Someone denounced him. When
he came back from the camp he was an old man . . .'
She must have sensed a stifled cry in him and guessed
that the pain did not come from the blows he had
received. 'I don't know why I started telling you all that.
Whatever you do, don't repeat it to anyone! Oh yes. I
was talking about the language of the camps . . .'

'She's afraid,' thought Elias. 'This young woman who
had the courage to intervene just now, is afraid.'

'So what did you say to those guys at the depot?' he
asked her, assuming a relaxed tone. Anna's voice responded casually, echoing his own: 'It was the fact that
I was talking the convicts' lingo that surprised them.
Not the sense of what I was saying. You see, what
mattered most of all to them was to put you down.
Human society's very similar to the animal world in
this respect. I've studied it on my ethology course. Except
that animals don't use words to injure one of their own
species . . . Here we are. We've arrived. Your hostel's
over there. Now I'm going to take the metro . . .'

She vanished into the white tempest. Elias took several steps, then ran to return her scarf to her and at the entrance to the metro stopped, stamping his feet amid the piles of snow. He felt himself becoming again what he was for that crowd of Muscovites: a tall black man, vaguely comic, his curly hair white with snowflakes.

He spent several days looking for her at Moscow University, wandering the corridors, waiting as they came out from lectures. This young woman's life, he understood, cast doubt upon that future world he had dreamed of. And yet it was she who gave this dream its simple, human and tragic truth.

'It's not the fact that she's beautiful . . .' He often began in this way without finishing his thought when, after he'd found Anna again, he picked her out amid the rowdy throng of the students. Hiding behind a pillar in the main hall of the faculty, he saw young women just as pretty and much better dressed than her. It was the start of the '70s, the first post-Stalin generation was coming up to the age of twenty . . . He watched them passing, attracted glances, sometimes amused, sometimes scornful (the whole range of these expressions was familiar to him). And suddenly this long, shapeless black coat, these old shoes, their heaviness jarring with the slenderness of the ankles. The face looked severe, almost hostile. The eyes, slanting towards the temples, resembled those of a she-wolf.

'No, it's not her beauty . . .' thought Elias and hastened to go outside, to make his way towards an empty pathway, knowing that very soon he would hear footfalls behind him and would recognize them. A hand would slip round his arm and they would plunge into the maze of little streets over which a winter dusk was falling.

So many things about her should have displeased him! Her clothes, more suited to the peasant women laden with bundles who jostled one another in the railway stations of Moscow. Her harsh voice, devoid of seductive musicality. The toughness that sometimes showed through the vulnerability of her youth.

With other women he had always known where he was going, what he expected of them and what they hoped for from him. With her . . . Anna clasped his arm and they began walking at random, or not entirely so, for she was showing him a Moscow he would never have discovered on any map. They spoke little, without any logic, looking at one another through the rippling of the snow, in silence, as if after years of separation.

Was he right to hide, to wait for her outside in these empty, snow-filled pathways? 'Like a meeting between secret agents,' he thought with a smile. She seemed to be grateful for his discretion. He was not unaware of what it signified in this country, the fact of 'going out with a black man'. Sometimes, on the other hand, she showed herself indifferent to what people might think of them as a couple. As on that evening when she stopped in a courtyard beyond the reach of the city's hubbub. They could hear the rustle of the snow against the windows and the slow, grave notes of a piano. On the first floor of a block of flats the interior of a vast room, dimly lit, pictures on the walls and the silhouette of the person playing. People were coming into the courtyard, crossing it, going up to their homes. A few of them turned back to satisfy themselves that this young woman and this African, motionless beneath the falling snow, were not a mirage. Elias felt Anna's fingers squeezing his hand. The life that could be guessed at behind the first-floor windows suddenly seemed to him very close to what the two of them could have lived together . . .

One day, when they were sitting in a tea shop he asked her, with a little nod towards the other customers: 'What do they think when they see us together?'

'If I tell you the truth you'll be upset . . .'

'Go ahead. I'm beginning to be immune.'

'Two schools of thought. The first think I'm simply a slut. The second think I'm a slut who wants to go abroad at any price. There . . . No, I almost forgot. There must be one charitable soul among them who thinks that in four generations a union such as ours might produce a new Pushkin . . .'

'You know one of our instructors puts it with a bit more humour. A countrywoman comes to Moscow. For the first time in her life she sees a black man. "Oh look, a monkey in the street!" The black man remarks politely: "No, citizen. I'm an African . . ." The countrywoman: "Ooh! And, what's more, it's a talking monkey" . . . After all, the Portuguese didn't think any differently when they cut our heads off in '61.'

'Let's leave! The way they're looking at us makes me feel as if I had glue on my skin. I feel dirty.'

'But why?'

'Because I used to think more or less the same as them!'

*   *   *

Humour often helped them. That glance, at once alarmed and confused, from a lady who found herself next to Elias one evening at the theatre. The lights went down and he whispered in Anna's ear: 'I'm going to tell her I've just been playing Othello and didn't have time to remove my make-up . . .' The actors were dressed as soldiers in the civil war and the stale dialogue matched the dust on their costumes. One of them declaimed ecstatically, rolling his eyes upwards: 'The fire of our revolution will give birth to the new man!' At the interval Anna suggested they leave.

The first snow squall restored them to the life they loved. They let themselves wander through the labyrinth of little alleys that had survived the follies of reconstruction, walked down to the frozen ponds in a park, hearkened to the wind lashing the turrets of a ruined monastery. The world reminded them of the play they had just fled: a pompous and loquacious farce forever shuffling its masks and its ham actors. Not to mention a certain lady in the eleventh row, contemplating the empty seat on her right with relief . . . They no longer needed that world.

What he felt was so simple he did not even try to put it into words. It was enough for him to be walking with her beneath the snow, to feel the warmth of her hand, then the absence of this hand, the icy scent of the air, and on the frozen window of a late and almost empty bus, to see the dark circle left by Anna's breath: she would peer through it from time to time, so as not to miss their stop, and that delicate trace of her breath would quickly become covered again with crystals of hoar-frost. When they got off it seemed to him as if that rickety bus was carrying away with it a very important fragment of their lives.

He now had a breathless attachment to things that had previously seemed insignificant, invisible. One day, as he waited outside the university cloakrooms, he noticed a black garment in the row of coats and immediately recognized its shape and tired fabric. This gloomy place, bristling with coat hooks, was suddenly filled with an intense and vibrant life for him, much more real than everything happening elsewhere in that great building groaning with marble. He went up to it and saw the last snowflakes were melting on the black coat's worn collar. So Anna had only just arrived for her lectures and the waiting period he must now endure seemed to him very different from the hours and minutes that passed for the others.

He had never lived through such moments in the company of a woman and indeed had never imagined himself capable of living and seeing with this grievous felicity, this hallucinatory sharpness. It was so new for him that one day he felt tempted to make fun of the extreme sensitivity he now felt within himself. 'The new man!' he declared, mimicking the costumed revolutionary in the play he had seen with Anna. He smiled but the description did not seem incorrect: an unknown being was coming to life within him. And when he thought about this new presence, an alloy of tenderness, confidence, peace and the terrible dread of losing what he loved, a memory came back to him whole: the threshold of a hut at nightfall and the child burying his face in the crook of his mother's arm.

He now believed he had found the one to whom he could speak of that child, whose existence he had so far never admitted to anyone.

For the moment the lecture theatre was empty. Elias walked right up to the back row, where not even the recalcitrant students bothered to climb. He lay down across the seats and followed the slow awakening of the room as an invisible witness: the first voices, still resonant and distinct, the thumping of bags on the desk tops, the rolling of a pen, an oath, then the crescendo of the uproar, laughter and, closer to his row, a tune being whistled, as if apart from the general cacophony. But, above all, that taut nerve within him, the timid hope of being able to make out Anna's voice amid all this talk. Finally the rapid diminuendo of the noise, the lecturer's abrupt, leonine cough, the practised rhythm of his percussive delivery.

Lying there, Elias could see the silent, tumultuous precipitation of the white flurries outside the high bay windows. He told himself that from time to time, as she looked up from her notes, Anna might also be noticing this snowy tempest.

'. . . Creatively and with genius, Lenin thus develops the Marxist theory of socialism. Employing arguments that are historically and logically incontrovertible, he demonstrates that the construction of a socialist society is possible within one country, even if it is surrounded by hostile capitalist neighbours . . .' Elias listened to the less tedious fragments, including this one, which, without the censorship he usually imposed on himself, provoked the thought: 'How true all that is. And how pointless . . .' Yes, incongruous in this universe where outside the windows dusk was slowly falling on a snowy day.

He knew that after these lectures Anna would stay behind in the lecture room for a few minutes to chat with a tall red-haired girl, her friend, who had transformed her first name into the somewhat improbable 'Gina'. On this occasion it seemed to be a conversation embarked on long before, for Anna was merely responding distractedly to Gina's unpleasant and vehement remarks.

'No, you do what you like,' Gina was saying. 'Look. When it comes to negroes, I know the score. He's nice enough today, your Congolese . . . right, Angolan, I mean. But don't forget. A black man's a rutting orangutan. And once he's screwed you it's *bye-bye baby!* And you'll be left with a little half-monkey on your hands. And taking pills for who knows how many tropical diseases . . .'

'Listen, Gina, we haven't got to that stage at all, him and me. And he's never . . .'

'OK, he hasn't got into your knickers yet, this saint. He's just biding his time, that's all. So it's down to you to choose your day. Yes, your day. He's polygamous like they all are down there. And it'll be your turn to get laid on, let's say, Wednesdays. After all the rest of the tribe . . .'

On his way there Elias had been planning to appear in front of them, leaping out from the row where he had hidden, to take them by surprise. He was hoping to get himself accepted by the red-headed Gina. He was even preparing to do his number, emitting the cry of a rutting orang-utan, when the true sense of this teasing suddenly became clear to him. All these taunts about the erotic excesses of black men were nothing more than folklore, to which he had long since become accustomed. The true question had the unvarnished and woeful banality of real life: after her studies Anna ran the risk of ending up in some remote corner of her native Siberia, so she must invent a means of remaining in the paradise of Moscow. Marry an African? Gina had considered this and arrived at her verdict: you'd be better off going and teaching Hegelian dialectics to the wolves in the *taiga* . . .

At a certain moment the argument began to go round in circles. Elias remained lying there and, with his head tilted slightly backwards, he saw the swirling of long plumes of snow around a street lamp. A simple and intense happiness was conjured up by this hypnotic movement. Their wanderings through Moscow beneath surges of white . . . The little circle of melted hoar-frost made by Anna's breath on the window of a bus . . . He closed his eyes, tried not to hear the two voices down at the bottom of the lecture theatre, discussing the pros and cons of his blackness.

Anna said very little, in fact. Elias thought he could make out the rather slow intonation that he often noticed when she was speaking. 'Look, Gina, of course he's black and all that. But he understands me like nobody else . . .' There was an exaggeratedly scornful laugh from Gina, the click of a lighter and this observation: 'You're

really stupid, my little Anna. Though . . . come to think
of it, maybe you're made for each other. He's just climbed
down from his baobab tree and you've just emerged
from your bear's den . . .' As if she had not heard, Anna
continued in the same dreamy tone: 'And then, don't
laugh, but he's a bit like a knight in shining armour!
Yes. You know, I read that poem a thousand times in
my teens. You remember. A lady drops her glove into
an arena full of lions and tigers. The beasts roar but
this knight goes to retrieve the glove and returns it to
the lady . . . Yes I know, I know . . . A childishly
romantic German poem . . . But you see, with him I feel
I'm never telling lies. While with Vadim everything
becomes false. Even the way I walk. With Vadim even
the snow smells like ice from the fridge . . .'

Elias saw this young man with Anna the following
evening. Thanks to the conversation in the lecture theatre
he knew that Vadim was a Muscovite, the son of a
senior government official. 'If I were you,' Gina had
yelled, 'I'd stick to him like a plaster. In two years' time
he'll have a diplomatic post abroad.' Elias had pictured
him as tall, arrogant, athletic, a worthy representative
of the capital's gilded youth. He detested him before
having seen him.

Vadim came into the entrance hall of the library and
for a few seconds was blinded. He took off his misted-
over spectacles, began wiping them and, with his myopic
eyes tightly screwed up, peered into the surrounding
haze. He was tall, with a slight stoop and a handsome
face spoiled by the childish softness of the lips. In taking
a handkerchief out of his pocket to wipe his glasses he

had dropped a small piece of card, no doubt his library ticket. He leaned forward, looking around him, still with this tentative, myopic air. Elias, who was watching the scene reflected in a mirror at the end of the entrance hall, had an impulse to go and help him . . .

Anna arrived at that moment, picked up the card, walked with Vadim to the exit. They paused a few yards away from Elias, who caught the young man's half-wistful, half-vexed words: 'No. You know, Mama's told me I've got to be careful about my bronchitis. Especially because out there, in mid winter . . .' They went out and Elias noticed that Anna's gait was indeed no longer the same: the measured steps you take alongside an old man.

Two days later he learned that during the holidays she would be going to her village in eastern Siberia. 'Perhaps I could . . .' It did not feel as if he were asking her, it was the echo of a dream finding expression almost without his knowing it. 'It takes seven days, and it can easily reach fifty below over there,' she replied, as if trying to dissuade him.

In the course of the umpteenth assault on the 'presidential palace' Elias stumbled, fell and sprained his foot. Having succeeded in making the doctor believe this, he gained an extra week of leave.

They set off just as the weather had turned warmer; Moscow smelled of damp turf. During the second night, in a station close to the Urals, Elias climbed down onto the footboard of the carriage and found he could not breathe. The frozen air had the cutting hardness of a crystal.

III

Extreme cold darkens the skin more than sunburn. Elias learned this from observing the Siberian who got onto the train at Krasnoyarsk. A face burned by chilblains, hands rutted with swarthy cracks. 'Aye. That's the true colour of gold,' the man joked, in response to Anna's quick glance. He was sharing a compartment with them. Out of his bag a meal appeared: an earthenware pot containing salted mushrooms ('We'll give them time to breathe, the brine's completely frozen'), smoked elk meat, a couple of pints of dark vodka infused with bilberries. He offered it, too, to an elderly woman who spent every day on her couchette opening and closing a little casket. He talked about his occupation, about extracting nuggets from the permafrost, about how his sleep was plagued by swarms of mosquitoes and the growling of bears. After the third glass he thumped Elias on the shoulder and proclaimed with warm, fraternal emotion, 'Last January when it was sixty below and windy as well, I turned blacker than you in the . . .' He was about to say 'face' but stopped himself and uttered a word that was incongruous, because too old-fashioned and poetic in the context, *lik*, more appropriate for the countenance of an icon.

Everyone laughed and Elias perceived the distance they had travelled since Moscow. His colour no longer made a monkey of him nor a propaganda symbol, nor a totem that required bowing and scraping from humanists. It was visible, of course, but just like the marks of frost on a face. All the man in his clumsy way wanted to say to him was: 'The fact that you're black is nothing. Worse things happen.' He talked about one of his comrades who had had an arm torn off by an excavator. The woman told them that what she was carrying in her casket was her husband's ashes, as well as the fragment of a shell that had remained in the old soldier's leg for thirty years . . .

They were drawing close to the limits of the empire, a place where brutalized lives run aground, human beings considered undesirable in the big cities. This end of the world blended together a multiplicity of ethnic groups and customs, a variegated universe that embraced this African as one more nuance in the chaotic mosaic of humanity. Elias would become aware of this later. For the moment he was trying to befriend a Buryat child, who was out in the corridor staring at him from the narrow slits of his eyes. 'Who am I for this child?' Elias wondered. 'Maybe simply the closest to what I am . . .'

At the start of the journey Anna seemed tense, vigilant over every word spoken. 'Travelling in the company of a black man, that's a bold exploit!' he thought, with a smile. The 'rutting orang-utan' came to mind and he guessed that she dreaded an even more extreme gesture, a remark that would put her on the spot. To be taken for a monster of lubricity amused him, especially since for days now the only question that had truly preoccupied him was how to explain what the scent of the snow in the folds of that grey woollen dress meant to him. And the footprints they left at a tiny remote station in the middle of the *taiga*. And the fragrance of the tea she brewed for him each morning. There was more truth in the headiness of these moments than in all the declarations of love in the world. But to say so would already have been a declaration.

The journey lasted so long that one evening he caught himself having forgotten its goal. Or rather the sole purpose of the endless pounding of the track was now these brief lapses into beauty, and he did not know how to talk about them to Anna.

She no longer seemed on her guard, far from it, Elias's attitude intrigued her. She was clearly hoping for something other than this friendly and attentively protective presence . . .

The woman with the casket left them at Irkutsk. The gold prospector at a village beyond Baikal. They found themselves alone, their eyes fixed on the fading of the sparks given off by the sunset outside the window layered with hoar-frost. The last night of their journey was beginning. Now they needed to talk, to clarify the situation, or else, without saying anything, embrace, exchange caresses, give themselves . . . Or instead, laugh, tell jokes, assume the role of good chums. Mentally they were rehearsing these scenarios, but all of them seemed false. The scarlet blaze on the window turned to violet, then was extinguished. There came a moment when it seemed impossible to turn away from the window, to meet one another's eyes and smile . . .

A light tapping on the door drew them out of this torpid state. The little Buryat boy was watching them fixedly, with slightly arched eyebrows, pursing his lips, in an expression that seemed to respond to the intensity of what he sensed in them . . . They exchanged glances and began to laugh softly. Yes, how could he make this young woman understand that the simple freshness of the snow, as it lingered on her dress, was already abundant happiness, a true love story that had unfolded ever since their wanderings through Moscow beneath storms of white? How could she tell this man that he had become important to her, strangely, despite all she thought about men, white or black, and all she believed about herself, tell him that his presence there was obvious and natural, as if he had been at her side long long ago beneath this Russian sky, as if he had always been there, and always would be? She thought he was like that aircraft from the last war set in a block of concrete in the city where she went to secondary school. It was the district where the city's worthies lived and there this Il-2 ground attack aircraft, nicknamed 'Black Death' by the Germans, proudly reared its dark, elongated silhouette, amid pretentious, humdrum lives . . . Anna suppressed a smile: this far-fetched comparison was perfectly apt but completely unmentionable, as apt things so often are.

The Buryat woman came and fetched her child. They were left in the blue dusk that filled the compartment.

'. . . In the end this is the one mystery that stays with me from my childhood. Even though my mother was crushed by poverty and the contempt of those who bought her body, she was able to give me absolute happiness, peace without any taint of anxiety. I've always believed that this capacity for love, which is, in fact, so simple, is a supreme gift. Yes, a divine power . . .'

During the last night of the journey he talked about that child on the threshold of a hut in Dondo burying his face in the crook of his mother's arm.

The following evening the declaration they had been waiting for finally arrived and was made wordlessly. Quite simply, they came close to death on the ice of a river which served as a road in winter. A lorry driver had left them at this intersection of forest roads. He had sworn his comrade would be along at any minute. It was still daylight. An hour later darkness enveloped the little shelter with three walls where they had taken refuge. They spent that hour jumping up and down, pummelling one another, rubbing one another's cheeks and noses. The air was clear, no breath of wind. The cold moulded itself to their bodies as if they were encased in molten glass. And once they moved, this carapace exploded and they felt as if they were swallowing crushed splinters.

They made a fire, but in order to fetch wood they had to climb a steep bank, plunge waist deep into the snow, battle with branches, using hands that no longer obeyed them. This expedition took a good twenty minutes, the fire had time to die down and their muscles to go numb, anaesthetized by the cold. At one moment, halfway between the shelter and the forest, Elias wanted to lie down, to sink back into the drowsiness that made him light-headed, unfeeling. He shook himself, snatched up a fistful of snow, rubbed his face furiously, then clambered up and, with gritted teeth, began breaking branches. And all at once stood upright, listened . . . As he came hurtling down the slope he lost half of the firewood. 'I heard . . . I heard . . .' he said in a whisper, as if his voice might alarm the faintly detected sound. They listened, turning their heads right and left. All that was perceptible was tiny crackling noises from the fire that had almost gone out. The mist from their breath rose upwards, drawn aloft by the black gulf of the sky. The stars seemed to be closing in on them, surrounding them . . . Elias felt the pressure of a hand on his wrist and could no longer make out whether he was giving or receiving the warmth that remained to them. Anna pressed herself against him and there amid the starry space they formed a frail islet of life.

The driver who picked them up would seemingly have remained just as impassive had he come upon their frozen corpses inside the shelter. Elias studied the hands resting on the wheel: fresh scratches, the blood scarcely dried, and showing through beneath it, a faint tattoo, 46–55 and the name of one of the camps at Kolyma.

The man spoke, offering no excuses but simply to establish what Elias already knew: 'Worse things happen.' Worse was the frosts that followed a brief thaw. The ice on the rivers he drove along became covered in water and this froze in its turn. One river on top of another, as it were. The wheels sank into it and in a matter of moments were caught, welded in. That was what had happened to him a little earlier. Sometimes lorries were discovered under six feet of snow . . . Between the two numerals on his tatto the computation was simple: 1946–1955, nine years of forced labour somewhere beneath this icy sky. 'After that,' thought Elias, 'nothing else can really touch him . . .'

'You should have come to Sarma in the spring,' lamented the driver suddenly. 'There's a spinney over there, half a dozen miles or so, full of birds. How they sing, the little buggers! Nightingales. You wouldn't believe it. Over there. Near where the camp was . . .' A minute later he began making little clacking noises with his tongue, followed by a whistling and clicking sound. Elias thought he was imitating the trilling of a nightingale. The driver growled: 'What a stupid bitch, that dentist! I told her to take it out. She's filled it, that bloody back tooth. And now I don't need a thermometer any more. As soon as it gets to forty below it has me howling like a wolf.'

As he dropped them at Sarma just after midnight, he whispered to Elias with a wink: 'You look a lot like Pelé. I saw him playing a couple of years ago, on television . . . Off you go. Stoke the stove well!' For a moment they watched the swaying of the long trailer laden with tree trunks. The sensation of parting from a man in the midst of this white infinity had a grievous intensity about it. 'Nine years in the camp, nightingales, a badly filled molar, Pelé . . .' Elias felt he had made contact, in a brief space of time, with the subterranean and tangled truth of a human being.

This intimacy with the truth, at once poignant and radiant, struck him more than everything else at Sarma. From the very first look Anna's mother gave him. She opened the door to them, put her arms round them, without wasted words, incuriously. A calm, absolute certainty was transmitted to Elias: he could walk in at this door in ten years' time and she would be waiting for him.

'The bath's still hot,' the mother said. 'In this cold, I knew you'd be late . . .'

To him everything in the tiny bath house was amazing: the bitter scent of the smoke-caked walls, the birch twigs with which he was expected to lash himself, the steam burning his nostrils. But this exoticism was nothing beside the blue darkness perceived through the narrow window above a bench. Outside the cloudy glass the cold forbade any trace of life, while here, on the planks drenched in boiling water, was his naked body, more alive than ever.

At Sarma he saw death, survival and life combining in a secret, constant transfusion.

He awoke dazzled by the abundance of sunlight. And the first thing he saw on this white planet was a dot moving slowly along in the middle of a valley surrounded by the *taiga*. A man? An animal? Elias watched the sinuous path followed by this little black speck, then made a tour of the room, looked for a long time at the photo of a young soldier. 'Smolensk, April 1941', it said at the bottom of the picture . . . The wooden front steps groaned loudly under someone's footsteps. Elias hurried into the entrance hall and saw Anna's mother. 'She's gone to see Georgi, the hunter, to fetch a good fur jacket for you. You won't get far with that coat of yours. It's forty-eight below this morning . . . Come and drink some tea.' The surface of the water in the two pails she set down was pearly with ice.

At table the silence that fell was not oppressive. The crackling of the fire, the drowsy ticking of a clock and, most of all, the great tranquillity, all this made words less necessary. And yet Elias felt he needed to give an account of himself, to explain his presence ('My African face,' he thought, vexed with himself for not finding any way to start a conversation). Then he remembered the driver who had given them a lift the night before, his tale of the nightingales . . . The woman listened to him then, after a moment's hesitation murmured: 'Yes. There used to be a lot of birds at the time when the camp was there. Yes. Nightingales more than anything . . . Then one day, at the end of the '40s, I think, the authorities gave orders to cut down all the trees. They'd noticed that in springtime, as soon as the birds began to sing, the number of escapes went up. Under Khrushchev they closed the camp. The trees have grown again. The birds have come back . . .'

Anna returned bringing a long fur jacket. 'There. Put that on and you can go into hibernation. It's bear.'

Outside, in the valley's blinding whiteness the same black speck continued its winding course. 'And that? Is that a bear too?' asked Elias. 'No. It's the student I told you about. Well, he's over fifty now. You remember, the one who wrote "SOSialism" . . . He's out searching for his treasures. But it'd be better for him to tell you about them himself. We'll go and see him this evening, if you like . . .'

Elias was expecting to find a madman undermined by the harshness of exile. The 'student' spoke with an irony which presumed a diagnosis along these lines and thus refuted it. 'To begin with,' he recounted, 'it was

just a schoolboy's bright idea. Most meteorites either
land in inaccessible places, oceans, seas, lakes or mountains, for example. Or else on rocky terrain where these
intergalactic visitors remain hidden amid the stones. So
this poor student (who was obliged, alas, to interrupt
his studies for a time) decided to search for heavenly
objects where they're most visible: on the immaculate
whiteness of our beloved Siberia. I have a hundred corres-
pondents more or less everywhere this side of the
Urals . . . And now take a look at my collection!'

In long cases squared off into compartments they saw
smooth fragments, some as small as cherry stones, some
bulkier, reminiscent of dark Stone-Age flints. On a large
table covered with a waxed cloth there was an accu-
mulation of chemistry apparatus, a star atlas, a telescope
on a tripod. The commentary that was now delivered
soon became at once too technical and too rhapsodic.
To follow it all one would have had to fall in love with
the tiniest streak on the surface of these aerolites . . .
The 'student' realized this, characterized himself as
'obsessed with stars' and, as if seeking their pardon for
his astronomical pedantry, proclaimed: 'I've even written
a poem . . .' He took down a sheet of paper that hung
above his work table, put on his glasses and began to
read. It was the tale of a meteorite hunter who
constructed a planet for himself from his finds and quit
the Earth. The tone was that of the verses one wrote
at the age of twenty. 'He stopped growing up at the
moment of his arrest,' thought Elias.

They were already at the door, poised to leave, when
the 'student' led them back into the room. 'You know,
I want to say this without any political inference. From

time to time the human race should judge itself from the point of view of these pebbles from heaven. That might make it less confident of its greatness . . .'

On the way back, as they passed through the 'valley of the meteorites', they each caught themselves distractedly glancing down at every dark stain. They laughed about it. 'You know, he's never talked like that to anyone before,' said Anna. 'You must have impressed him. Yes. Like an extraterrestrial he can finally confide in . . .'

The next day at the edge of the *taiga* they came upon a couple who appeared to be seeking to bury themselves under the snow. An elderly man, dressed in a simple quilted jacket, a woman with slanted eyes, probably a Yakut. 'Are you digging a den?' Anna called out to them. 'Yes, a den for a flower,' replied the man. 'This time they won't go and trample on it.' He went back to thrusting long poles obliquely into the snow. Grasping the principle of this strange scaffolding, Elias helped them to complete it. They all went back together. The man told them that for years he had been watching out for the flowering of the 'golden fire', a kind of wild orchid, which opens at night and dies at dawn. He had located the spot where it grew but each time he had missed the night when it bloomed. Once winter was over the plant was often found trampled or uprooted by animals. So he had decided to construct a shelter before the snows melted . . .

They spent a while in the *izba* where the couple lived, ate some of the smoked fish prepared by the woman. The man was very eager to offer Elias a *shapka*. 'I've got five of them. I used to hunt a bit in the old days . . .

Choose which one you like. Not that one. That's a museum piece. I wore it at the camp. Well, I got through several over twenty years. This is the last of them. And as for the flower, the golden fire, I mean, it was a thief who told me where to find it. A gold washer, in point of fact. He used to work with his panning trough in secret. He was caught and for this he got ten years in the camp. Then one day in spring he tried to make a run for it. They tracked him down and the guards had dogs, as big as wild boar, that tore his throat out . . . He often used to talk to me about the flower, so, straight off, I began to imagine I might find it one night when I was free. And now, you see, I tell myself, it was that plant that helped to stop me losing my mind. Because over twenty years there was plenty to make you do that. Especially when I got to thinking about the price I'd paid for three cartloads of muck. You know the story, Anna, but what you don't know is that in '56, when I came out, they'd already chucked Stalin on the scrap heap. Then this fellow says to me: "Come on, Ivan. Take his picture and throw it on the dunghill. That way you'll be quits." Well, I didn't do it. Because now anyone could do it. Besides, I don't like to kick a man when he's down. And most of all, I couldn't care less. I'd already started looking for the golden fire . . . Now then. One more glass so you don't catch cold when you go out.'

They went home, cutting through the forest. Anna's words sounded like an echo lost among the great cedar trunks. 'When he met his wife, Zoya, she was . . . well, a kind of stray dog. Worse than a dog, a sick, half-mad wild animal, whom everyone despised. There are mines fifty miles away from Sarma. For a time the miners shared Zoya between them. When they went to work they locked her up in a shed and when they came back they raped her. In fact it wasn't even rape by then, more like a regular routine . . . Then they got rid of her. Yes, a dog rooting among rubbish. One evening Ivan was passing close by the miners' huts and, in the darkness, he thought he saw a fox. He was about to shoot it with his gun. Zoya was wearing an old coat scorched by fire . . . It took her several months to get back on her feet again. And one day Ivan told me he now knew why he went on living. And it was above all for her that he wanted to see that plant flowering in the night, the golden fire . . .'

Before making the journey, Elias had thought he would be encountering human detritus, left over from the great workshop of the future society. Offcuts, waste products, inevitable in a project on as grand a scale as that of communism. Yet here, among the materials rejected by the march of History, behold, a secret, tenacious life maintained its vigil. This humble existence seemed perfectly emancipated from the capricious rhetoric of the age. No verdict of History, thought Elias, had made its mark on these two beings who, when spring came, would be searching in the forest for their wild orchid.

One morning he saw Ivan leaving his *izba* and, a moment later, Zoya running after him. The man must have forgotten the leather bag she was holding out to him. She was dressed only in a skirt and pullover, despite the cold having gone down to fifty below, and this run through the snow, the encounter between the two figures in the middle of a white wilderness, their swift embrace, the tenuousness of the bond created between them for a moment, then broken, all this struck Elias as total evidence of love. 'A stray dog,' he recalled. 'Human offcuts . . .' Yet now in the silvery cold of the morning, there was this woman on the threshold of her house and this man, gliding along on his snow shoes, tracing an extended blue line across the endless white expanse.

Almost nothing was left of the camp. The shells of huts. The gap-toothed lines of a double wooden perimeter fence. It shook in the wind and from a distance it was possible to believe that an Alsatian dog was still trotting round between the twin palisades.

They approached with uneasy caution, not knowing what could be said at such a place. Thousands of lives swallowed up by this enclosed space between the watchtowers. Thousands of pairs of eyes staring, long ago, at barbed wire, all downy with hoar-frost under a cloudless sky. Were cries of pity called for, or indignation, or resignation? Words lost their meaning here. From a blackened pole hung a steel bar, the gong which had once marked the rhythm of the camp's activities. Its silence, perpetual now, was like an invisible but still living presence.

Elias listened to the wind, the crunching of their feet, pictured the man Anna had just been speaking about: one sunny day a prisoner clad in a worn quilted jacket leaves the camp, stops, looks back, perplexed. After twelve years of imprisonment, freedom is a threat. His body, worn out by penal servitude, betrays him at every step. He finds it hard to understand the people he passes, their smiles, their concerns. 'You should have remarried,' he says to his wife. He is terrified by that wait of twelve years. Terrified and sorrowfully grateful. He would like to thrust this woman away from him, thrust her towards joy, towards the youth she had lost on his account . . . He dies a year after the birth of their daughter. As a child, Anna will claim she remembers her father's face. It is, of course, impossible. She has simply seen old photos . . .

Elias noted the moment when the cold suddenly ceased. They walked round the camp, entered a wood of black alders. He took off his scarf and no longer felt the wind's cutting edge. The young woman facing him seemed breathtakingly close, known to him, as no one had ever been in his life before. He even thought he could recall the voice of the child she had been! As well as all those winter days she had lived through before they met. With the faith of a believer, he guessed at the sadness and beauty of what her eyes remembered. And, like an intoxication, he sensed the silence of the house where, as a small child, she would observe a beam of light from the setting sun on the picture of a soldier, then a branch covered in hoar-frost turning blue outside the window . . . Now, with the same intensity, he felt at one with the suddenly milder air Anna was breathing, and with the roughness of the bark lightly touched by her hand . . .

These were the trees the camp authorities had had cut down to put an end to the birdsong. Elias looked up: high above them the bare branches, encrusted with ice jewels, rang softly in the wind, like an echo of the warbling of long ago . . . his *shapka* slipped, fell into the snow. He picked it up but was in no hurry to put it on, he was so hot.

'I'm here at last . . .' the notion took shape, confused, yet expressing vividly what was happening to him. The serene truth of his presence here, in this place of forgotten evil, in the dazzle of a snowy plain, beside a young woman, thanks to whom everything on this day was turning out to be of the essence of things, even the simple beauty of the tips of her eyelashes silvered with hoar-frost. Life was becoming as it ought to be.

'Mother comes here once a year, at the beginning of June,' Anna said. 'On the anniversary of my father's death. She spends the night here. I came with her once. When you hear the birds you don't really believe in death any more and it feels as if he can hear them too . . . Wrap up well. It's time to go home.'

He felt at one with every tree, with every glint of the low sun on the snow. Or rather he felt at one with himself in that day, which seemed always to have been waiting for him, and into which he was finally returning. Anna's hand, adjusting his scarf for him, emerged out of a very old memory, heady with tenderness. He grasped her fingers, pressed them to his face, closed his eyes . . . When they continued on their way he unbuttoned his coat, the air seemed to him balmy, aromatic. And already in the darkness on the outskirts of Sarma, his breath became so scorching that he felt that with one puff he could have warmed up all the ancient, chilled *izbas* of the hamlet.

That night, amid the furnace of his fever, a moment of great limpidity burst forth. 'I love her . . .' he admitted to himself with disarmed simplicity. Anna was standing on the threshold of the room.

Next day, the eve of their departure for Moscow,

Anna's mother gave them the money the people of Sarma had collected so that they could return by plane.

During the nine hours that the flight lasted, breathless from his illness, Elias swung between an absolute certainty of happiness and an awareness of never being able to recapture the radiance of that other life briefly glimpsed. It would have meant returning to Sarma, to live there with Anna in perpetual, humble, slow joy, rhythmed by the ebb and flow of the seasons. His cough had him by the throat, he was breathing like a hunted animal and told himself that Anna had done everything in her power to escape those long, somnolent winters, the bleak memory of the dead. No, he would have had to take her to the islands of Luanda beneath the sun, redolent of the warm algae and the hot timber of the boats. He sat up in his seat and began to talk of the fishermen, silhouetted against the sunsets, of the woman, his mother, waiting for their return. They would go and settle there, she would love the country . . . Suddenly he remembered who he was: a young African, stateless, a half-monkey to those who occupied Angola. The tangled knot that derived from these thoughts drew ever tighter. At one moment Anna's face appeared to him shrouded in darkness, unrecognizable. Who was she, in fact, this woman offering him a pill and a glass of water? Was it she who had paused in the midst of endless snows and made alive and necessary every moment that passed? Or a young woman from the provinces who wanted to stay in Moscow at all costs? And what was there to be done about the scent of hoar-frost that her dress exhaled when she climbed back into the train? And about the poem she had loved in her youth: a knight going down into the arena among the big cats and retrieving the glove a lady had let fall? And about the child in a silent *izba*, talking to the photo of a soldier? . . .

He felt profound pity for this child, now grown into an adult. Instead of the scraps of dreams he could offer her, she ought to do everything possible to succeed in Moscow, far from those endless winters, from those phantom camps. She ought to marry this Vadim, this nice, gentle Daddy's boy. If only that could make her happy . . .

Had he said all that in a moment of delirium? Had she replied? At all events it was during the flight that she told him her secret: to be admitted to the university she had lied and told them her father had been killed in the war. She lived in fear of being unmasked, sent back, ending up in Sarma . . .

Towards evening, during a few minutes of calm, he looked out of the window. Barely tinged with pink by a dull sun, a uniform white expanse lay there, the same ever since their departure. The freedom of these spaces was intoxicating, gave one the desire to travel through them in every direction, to land anywhere, to take off again. And yet amid this immensity Anna's life traced a fragile line, suspended from a lie, stretched between this dreamed-of Moscow and the ice hell of her native village. A little like the glimpses of a road down below, amid fields under snow.

She came to see him every day while he was convalescing. They spoke little, disconcerted by the doomed nature of the choice that their trip had just laid bare:

Moscow, Sarma, a calculated happiness here, at the cost of renouncing an improbable happiness back there. Destiny, a precise line that must be followed without deviation. Brave daydreams, wretched common sense. And the scent of the forest in winter clinging to a woman's clothes as she climbs back on board a train . . .

One day, with the vigour of restored health, he talked about the struggle that could change the face of the world, about playing a part in History . . . Anna listened to him, made a little uneasy by his enthusiasm. Then he realized that she had been born and lived in a country that had turned History into a divinity and sacrificed millions of lives to create a new humanity. He was disconcerted to realize that what he liked the most in this new world was the very debris of those old lives that had been sacrificed, the 'human detritus', the people of Sarma . . . It was among these outcasts that he had found true fraternity . . .

He tried to explain this to Anna and received a reply that was very just in its cruel candour: 'You see, the people who live at Sarma don't expect anything more from life. Perhaps that's what makes them fraternal. They're not . . . how can I put it . . . They're not hungry. But I expect a great deal more from my life. Yes, I'm hungry. Later on, perhaps . . .'

For a long time Elias would retain in his memory the paradox of this hunger, which obliges us day after day to fritter away an existence we know to be false and empty, while the radiance of quite a different life is already known to us.

* * *

When the training sessions resumed again, he would reflect during the assault on the 'presidential palace' that this scenario of revolution offered a perfect summation of human History: fine words, the thrill of battles and enmities, victories greedy for corpses, and, when it's all over, far away from the victors, this calm, grey winter's day, the scent of a wood fire, the intense sensation of being at one with oneself.

During his absence, the celluloid doll that marked the children's room in the 'palace' had lost its frilly dress and looked more than ever like a dead baby.

IV

Just as he was preparing to leave the 'presidential palace', the chief instructor told Elias to follow him. 'There are people in Moscow who want to talk to you . . .' he informed him sombrely. Pointless to ask for more details, this secretive mentality was well known to him.

After an hour in a car they found themselves in an office containing monolithic wooden furniture and an abundance of telephones, as if to emphasize that serious matters were afoot. As two individuals greeted Elias without the faintest hint of a smile, the instructor melted into the background. From the first few moments he sensed that this conversation would be more a game of symbols than a genuine exchange. He, the simple young African, was going to have the privilege of glimpsing the machinery of Soviet power. They were going to dub him, to invest him with a mission . . . The two men, one tall and massive, who looked like a grizzled mastiff, the other dry and athletic, were not very forthcoming. 'The interventionist aims of the USA', 'our military assistance to the forces of liberation', 'the Portuguese colonialists', 'probing the secrets of the enemy', a few such set phrases merely formed the spoken framework for the scene. What was important was focused on the silence of the chief instructor, who had suddenly become a subordinate, the ringing of a telephone and the grave reply of the grey-haired man. 'Yes. We'll be drafting a special report for the Politburo.' But, above all, on the almost rock-like rigidity of these bodies, the calm ponderousness of gestures and looks designed to embody the unshakeable strength of the regime. And it was only at the end, when everyone stood up, that the man-mastiff allowed himself a more informal tone of voice: 'Things will be hotting up soon in your Angolan homeland. We must be prepared. We'll need you, young man . . . The commander,' he nodded towards the instructor, 'will give you all the details . . .'

Elias was about to discover that these 'details' encompassed the training he would receive as a future intelligence agent, his involvement in subversive operations undertaken in Africa and, quite simply, his whole life, which from now on belonged to the Cause. The arrogant solemnity of the two individuals who had informed him of this, without even consulting him, infuriated him. But at once he recalled that these orders emanated from a power capable of flattening the world a thousand times over with nuclear thunderbolts. And that it confronted another, American, power, equally capable of incinerating the planet. And that in this struggle, in which man had long since been left behind, it might be possible to become a tiny cog, turning in the direction of good. And that for him this good would be for his homeland to become one where there were no longer cities out of bounds to black people.

The months that followed made of him what, as an adolescent, he used to dream of being: a professional revolutionary. What he would be until his death, in fact. Yet when talking to me about that training period, he would tell me: 'You know I became the kind of black man who runs the risk of bursting with the sense of his own importance. One of those Africans who wrinkles his nose up as if the whole world smelled bad. Fortunately some of the comrades with whom I was due to land in Angola were even more puffed up than me. It was really ridiculous. It sobered me up . . .'

What brought him down to earth in particular was the serene and pitiless fatefulness of his love for Anna. He was unable to tell her about the direction his life was now taking but, not without a certain exultation, he gave her to understand that future horizons of dangers and battles in unknown lands were opening up before him. She listened to him in silence, attempting an uneasy smile. Very briefly he experienced a mixture of pity and triumphalism, that infamous combination, which is present to a varying degree in all love. He at once felt ashamed, embraced Anna and swore he would return to her, despite continents separating them. He truly believed in this promise.

Years later he would recall that brief moment of boastfulness and his hasty repentance. He had never been superstitious, but that was the day, he would later tell himself, when his love for Anna, if it were to be preserved, should not have been tarnished by even that tiny degree of infamy. And she herself would much later confess to him that when she heard him talking about his likely departure for foreign lands she had resolved to die rather than return to Sarma . . .

But that March evening he believed they were bound to be together always, wherever it might be. For Anna, too, this seemed so vibrantly evident that she murmured these confused words, as if half in a dream: 'You may have to live far away and go for a long time without seeing me, but we'll still feel we're together, won't we?' These clumsily whispered words were at once a declaration of love and a premature farewell.

From that evening onwards everything came in a rush. History bolted: within a few weeks the dictatorship in Portugal collapsed and there was increasing talk of decolonization in Angola very soon. Elias remembered the two individuals who had dubbed him. They, too, must have been caught napping by the speed of events. The training he was undergoing was accelerated, he was introduced to the people who would, sub rosa, be 'leading the leaders' in the People's Republic of Angola, the future of which was already being written in Moscow. One of these eminences grises, who went by the name of Joâo Alves, took him out to lunch several times. Once again Elias felt himself to be 'an African wrinkling his nose up . . .'

He was in this mode the evening he went to Anna's birthday party. For this her friend Gina had lent her the room she rented in the suburbs. Coming out of the metro station he slipped on an icy section of pavement and brushed against a group of adolescent youths who were smoking and squabbling around a street kiosk. He ought not to have responded to their curses, should have lowered his head, made off. He stopped, tried to explain. Blows rained down on him, not particularly powerful or well directed, a hail of fisticuffs provoked by the unusual victim. They snatched at the bouquet, which he first tried to protect, knocked off his *shapka*. Their brutality was different in kind from the aggression at the train depot. Then he had sensed the hatred of mature men. On this occasion these were lean young layabouts, whose hands were blue with cold. For them brawling was almost a game, a way of keeping warm. They walked away from him just like children grown weary of an amusement. The whole gang of them abruptly abandoned the attack and ran off towards a more engaging distraction . . . He felt his face, his nose and lips were bleeding. The trampled flowers lay strewn across the snow. Two buttons were missing from his coat. A little boy walking along with his mother pointed his finger at the tall black man, mopping himself with a handkerchief stained red. Elias had an impulse to thrust both of them out of his way, then turned aside and had to make an effort not to weep.

He went home on foot, muttering reproaches, cursing the country, the slow pace at which the new man was coming into being here, and the stupid knight-errant role he had just been playing. He inveighed against Anna, her resignation, and Moscow, this crushing and cold city, the Russians and their past as slaves. And yet it was this past that made them close to him. In the end he found bitter consolation in telling himself that in Angola he would know how to avoid all the errors he had observed in the USSR. And that the Angolan revolution would be tarnished with none of these hereditary blemishes.

Their paths crossed on two occasions during the time before his departure (he concealed the episode of the brawl from Anna, invented a mission to a military camp in the provinces). The first time he did not notice her. It was she who told him about the scene later: he was coming out of a restaurant with an extremely elegant man (it was Alves) and a pretty, laughing woman (the latter's wife), they were getting into a foreign make of car and Gina, who was with Anna that day, gave a whistle: 'There you go, my poor friend, still running after your black prince. But you can see for yourself. He'd rather be screwing that chick with the stiletto heels . . .'

The second time, as if in a mirror image, it was Elias who, after two hours of waiting in the university foyer, came upon Anna, accompanied by Vadim and an elderly man (the young man's father, he was later to learn). Anna was weeping, Vadim was waving his arms about as if to drive away a wasp. The father, with a concerned but determined air, was talking in reassuring and controlled tones. For a brief, fantastic moment the trio reminded Elias of those trios of times past, arranged marriages where suddenly the fiancée bursts into tears. But no. It was actually a family matter in which he had no part to play.

They were left with this double misunderstanding for more than a month, then in a few minutes' telephone conversation he spoke to her about João Alves and Anna told him about the anonymous letter that had reached the rector of the university: in it she had been described as the daughter of a common criminal. By using all his connections, Vadim's father had managed to suppress the affair . . .

*   *   *

He was due to leave from a military airport to which she could not have access. They spent the evening of the previous day walking slowly along the sleepy alleyways between the Moskova and the Yauza rivers, amid the early April mist. Their lives had already diverged greatly and would continue to draw further apart, soon having no point of intersection at all. The torment of wars and African revolutions he was to plunge into. The life of the Moscow elite she would have to face up to. And yet that evening these destined life courses seemed to have no connection with their real lives. What was essential had already been found, they carried it within themselves, sharing it. At the moment of parting they did not embrace, they simply looked at one another for a long while. 'You know,' he said, 'we'll go back to Sarma one day and we'll find that orchid under the snow . . .'

In actual fact he did not speak of that return, for fear of making her cry. Simply, throughout the remaining years of his life, at the most painful times during all those years, he would repeat these words, like a silent prayer, which was known to no one but Anna.

V

In April 1977 in a street in Luanda he overheard a couple talking. The man was explaining to his wife that she was wrong not to clean the frying pan straight away after supper because the grease, when congealed, gave off an intolerably pungent smell of burnt fat. As man and wife walked along they continued their mild altercation, each half-heartedly rejecting the other's arguments. Given the price of oil, the woman maintained, it was better to keep a layer of it at the bottom of the frying pan . . .

A ridiculous echo struck a chord within him: Cuba, a young French *pasionaria* irritated by the increasingly bourgeois attitudes of the 'popular masses', forever frying their fish amid acrid oil smoke . . . Now in Angola it was Year III of the revolution. He glanced at the couple as they made their way along the Avenida Dos Combatentes. The husband, probably a member of the MPLA, the wife, given how she spoke and dressed, a government official. Both of them quite young. Sad.

The Portuguese had cut and run, the country belonged to the Angolans, areas out of bounds to blacks no longer existed. The intoxication of the brand new revolution was there to turn every word, every step taken into an adventure, a blaze of fire! 'If the revolution doesn't change the way we love . . .' Elias smiled, recalling the exalted dreams of his adolescence. In the distance the couple were still arguing: the man gesticulating with his right hand, no doubt demonstrating the correct way to scour a frying pan.

The intoxication was something he had experienced powerfully as soon as he returned. All the more because the revolution's success had proved to be almost unbelievably dazzling. The colonizers had packed their bags and left, and the MPLA, the Marxist-Leninist party (the only party, according to malicious tongues), had set about building the society of the future. In order to comprehend this rapid progress he had re-read a book on the 1917 revolution and verified that the seizure of power had been just as miraculously simple in Russia. Was this a trap set by History for revolutionaries drunk with victory?

He was reminded of this trap when he encountered the spouses discussing their frying pan. Year III of the revolution . . . He was on his way back from Zaire after an intelligence mission in the absurd war ('a weary war', he told himself) that put the two countries in conflict. The Angolan government wanted to know how much weight former refugees from Katanga carried in this struggle. The Soviets, for their part, were interested in the possibility of undermining Mobutu's regime. Out in the field this curiosity on the part of both had led Elias to an Angolan soldier who was slaking his thirst, his face immersed in the water of a river. Drawing closer, he had seen that the man was dead and little fishes were playing around his head as the current washed over it.

In the forest beside the riverbank the corpses there, too, had had time to settle into the poses of the living. That is how a battlefield appears when one comes upon it after the fighting is over . . .

He had been hit himself by a shell splinter: that streak above his left eyebrow. 'I could really have done without this trademark,' he told himself angrily. This nick was a characteristic feature of his image as a 'generic African'. As he looked in the mirror it suddenly occurred to him that this eyebrow, drawn into a slight frown by the scar, might be seen one day by Anna . . . For a long time now he had made it a rule to remember only one aspect of that Russian past: the train, that halt in the middle of the snowy *taiga,* a young woman climbing back on board, carrying the fragrance of the night in the fabric of her dress . . . In his profession the drug of memories was a grave danger, on account of their sweetness.

The argument about a badly cleaned frying pan was a trigger, both ludicrous and timely. He noted others, just as superficial and serious. For a time he managed not to grant them the terminal significance of: *When Revolutions Die . . .*

'The death knell sounds,' he thought one evening at an official dinner, 'when this type of woman appears.' Seated opposite him, the wife of one of the party leaders was puffing out her cheeks to suppress a belch, sighing, using a fork to toy with the food left on her plate. Year III of the revolution and somewhere, beside a river that young dead soldier and, on the opposite bank, a village where the children would have been at one another's throats for the meal that this fork was tinkering with . . .

Another sign, the impeccably dialectical slanging match between Joâo Alves, now a minister, and an army sergeant: unable to resolve which of them should end up with a fine car that had been smuggled into the port of Luanda.

But perhaps revolutions die when people begin going to visit them like private views at galleries. That tall Belgian woman, his father's girlfriend in Kivu. Louise Rimens, going to Havana as a revolutionary tourist. And now these armchair viewers of the march of History, the Europeans he encountered in Luanda.

In the month of May he forgot about these tiny indications that the revolutionary ideal was flagging. A popular uprising against the MPLA erupted. President Neto suppressed it in a bloodbath. This crackdown on 'factionalists' did away with a number of Elias's friends. 'The death knell sounds,' he told himself, 'when revolutionaries start killing one another,' and he was by no means certain of his own survival. His control, who dealt with the Soviet secret service, broke off all contact. Moscow was waiting to see how far the repression would go: should its agent be rescued from the Angolan quagmire or should he be sacrificed?

Elias was spared. 'Young but promising,' he quipped bitterly. The Soviets renewed contact and gave him a new mission: to gain authorization to be present at the interrogation of the 'factionalists'. He succeeded. In one cell he saw a woman lying unconscious. Beneath her torn dress broken ribs stuck out.

He recalled that President Neto wrote poetry.

In 1978 Elias formed a part of the Angolan delegation that accompanied Neto to Zaire. This visit to Mobutu by the Marxist president infuriated the Kremlin. Doubtless the countdown had now begun for Agostinho Neto, the poet, Elias thought . . . An odd journey, in the course of which Elias noted with astonishment that the soldiers polishing Marshal Mobutu's car were using French eau de toilette in spray form to clean the hub caps.

In May 1979 he again went to Kinshasa with a team that was to prepare for the new Neto-Mobutu summit. It was there that he learned of the arrest of Antonio Carvalho, the vet from Dondo who had made him read Marx. The man had now retired to the north of the country, playing no part in politics. But the hunt for 'factionalists' had a need to unmask enemies everywhere.

Elias left Kinshasa by car, travelling via Kikwit, hoping to reach Lunda Norte the following day. He was held at the frontier, not by the Zairean guards but by the Angolan rebel soldiers of UNITA. All things considered, the cruel tortures they inflicted were futile because the truth they were trying to extract from him was hard to admit: as one of Neto's men he was entering Lunda Norte to rescue someone Neto was going to kill.

They threw him into a wattle-and-daub hut and left him without water for a day and a half. He lost consciousness several times and came to during the second night when through the mists of his pain he heard whispering in a language he knew. He made an effort to prise open his eyelids, saw two shadows moving in the darkness. Two men the soldiers had recently impounded in this prison with crumbling walls. A dull voice muttered curses

Human Love

directed at the UNITA soldiers, then modulated into
snoring. A different, younger one, suddenly murmured
very distinctly: 'I want to die another way, not like this
African . . .' In Russian.

The young prisoner was afraid, Elias sensed his panic in the darkness. He was moved by this anxiety on the part of a foreigner, possibly on his first visit to Africa. He would have liked to reassure him, speak to him about an exchange of prisoners such as the UNITA military must have in mind, otherwise they would have killed all three of them . . . Along with the peasants they had just shot. He did not have the strength to say it, or even to make a sign to the Russian. His hands and feet were bound with wire that cut into his skin. But the will to assist the other man helped him to remain on the alert himself.

The soldiers' voices reached them through the unglazed window. He realized they were engaged in raping a woman. That fat Zairean woman with a very childish, chubby face whom he had noticed just before being thrown into this 'prison' hut . . . The young Russian stood up to peer at what was happening outside. One of the soldiers must have seen him, the door opened, thick boots began kicking, somewhat blindly, at the three bodies lying there. The young man shielded his head like a boxer on the ropes. His older comrade knew how to absorb the blows by means of abrupt, muscular swerves of his trained body.

Elias pictured the impression this must be making on

the young prisoner who kept whispering a mixture of curses and lamentations at intervals in the darkness. He probably perceived a world cleanly divided into the bastards, these UNITA brutes, who raped and killed and sold themselves to the Americans, and the heroes, or at least people of good will, struggling to guide Africa along the prescribed path of History. Yes, a clear and well defined perception of this kind. Tempting clarity . . .

Such a world, neatly cut in two, did not exist, Elias knew well. This night alone was an inextricable tangle of lives, deaths, words, desires, abysses. There was that woman with her childlike face and her heavy, fleshy buttocks, whom the soldiers were taking it in turns to violate. By diverting their aggression, this rape had very likely saved the three prisoners from being executed. Anyone skilled at telling fortunes would have shown that their survival depended simply on the pleasure offered by the buttocks of a woman on all fours beneath the soft light of the moon. And on the same night, in the town Elias had failed to reach, an old man, the vet, Carvalho, was being tortured to death. And on the beaten earth floor of a hut there lay this tall African ('me' he thought, in surprise), a virtual corpse, in fact, its wounds swarming with insects. In his youth this African had seen a man stretched out in a prison court-yard under a blazing sun, whose body presented more or less the same fly-infested wounds. The boy had made a silent vow then to fight against this world where a man could be transformed by his fellow human beings into such verminous flesh. The boy had grown up and fought and now this echo of the past was so cruelly droll as to make him smile, in spite of the pain.

'Men invoke History, politics, morality . . . This allows them to explain everything. The leader of UNITA, the wicked Jonas Savimbi, is supported by the wicked Marshal Mobutu, who is supported by the wicked American imperialists. And the MPLA's good President Agostinho Neto, supported by Moscow, is fighting these terrible people so that the ideals of fraternity may triumph. How clear it all is!'

Elias opened his eyes: amid the stifling density of the night that drunken child was putting his head through the window frame from outside and threatening the prisoners with a sub-machine gun. He was capable of squeezing the trigger for sport or in a simple muscular twitch. His face was rigged out in a gas mask with a torn-off tube. The glass was broken and his misty, drugged eyes appeared, now full of hate, now languid, like those of a sick child. For men who liked clarity this gaze did not exist.

Just as this African's racing thoughts did not exist ('me' Elias again reflected in amazement, and felt detached from the body covered in bleeding wounds, from the voice that was still alert within him). Two months earlier, that encounter at a diplomatic shindig in Lusaka. Anna with her husband, who now held a post at the Soviet Embassy. A young woman very much at her ease amid the absurd exchanges of social chit-chat. More beautiful than before, more radiant. And her Vadim who still had a slight stoop, a mild myopic air. Avoiding them had not been difficult . . .

The child appeared at the window again, aimed the gun, waved it. 'Shoot! Go ahead, shoot!' Elias caught himself thinking and was angry with himself for this weakness. But nevertheless the picture crossed his mind: a burst of gunfire, a moment of pain, that puts an end to the long drawn-out pain of a day and a half, erases Anna's face, whose new-found beauty is a betrayal of the face he loves. And after that burst, nothingness, which can only be the fragrance of the snow in the folds of a grey woollen dress . . .

He came to his senses on hearing a cry. A woman's voice, a brief exclamation, as if of joy, then the gunshot. Despite the throbbing of the blood in his temples he picked up what the soldiers were saying: the Zairean woman they had just shot had diamonds concealed in her mouth . . . The young Russian was at the window again. Elias guessed what he could see. A dead woman, a soldier extracting tiny grey granules from her mouth.

Then it came to him that the only true view of the world was precisely this one: in the dense humidity of a certain night men cluster around a woman who has just died, gripping her still warm body, which they have all had their way with. Unhurriedly, one of them rummages in the woman's mouth with his index finger, the moon is almost full (clarity!), a drugged child sleeps, leaning against a tree, and in towns and villages a few dozen miles away life continues, people prepare to go to bed, in Luanda a couple discuss the fat left in a frying pan, in Lusaka a young woman sleeps beside her diplomat husband whom she has never loved, in Paris a female intellectual writes a text about the betrayal of revolutions, while beneath the mud of the Russian plains, beneath the rocky American deserts, gigantic cylinders sleep, crammed with death and capable of taking off at any moment and obliterating this land bathed in the blue light of the moon. And at the very heart of this insane world there is respite, a wooden house, a woman who walks out onto the snow-covered front steps at nightfall and gazes at the white road below the terraced treetops of the dark *taiga* . . . He could knock on the door of that house tomorrow and he would be welcomed as if he were returning forever.

For a moment longer he succeeded in seeing the world thus, in the totality of its interconnected lives. Then his vision became blurred, such a perception was unendurable for one human being. His eyes had only borne it because death was at hand and this made him more than a man.

Feverish whispers already seemed to be reaching him from the far side of life. He moved his head and the pain from a cut reopening in his shoulder woke him up. 'Why are they taking so long to kill her?' Elias recognized the Russian's voice, words distorted by fear. He again wanted to reassure him, tell him about the Cuban commandoes who would doubtless attack at dawn (the previous day he had heard their gunfire, the kind of gunfire that draws the enemy into responding, thus giving itself away). He was going to survive, that young man, perhaps even to end up with a vivid memory of this night: the intimacy with death, a glimpse of madness, and then that dead woman spewing out diamonds . . . Scenes for a book he might well write in later life, as white people do, to draw a line under their years in Africa. In these pages everything would be clear. Heroes, villains. And everyone would have a life story that began at point A to arrive at point B. 'And yet when death stares you coolly in the face, you realize that in your life there are just a few hours, of sunlight or of darkness, a few faces, to which you return continually even as you draw further away from them . . .' Fishermen on the island of Cazenga, a woman waiting for them. Then the same woman sitting on the threshold of a hut, a child crouching at her knee, his face buried in the crook of his mother's arm. Then that moment when he was most intensely himself: a halt at a little station in the snow, a young woman climbing onto the footboard of a train . . . And that winter dusk, too, an elderly woman standing on the front steps of her house, watching a bend in the road . . .

He regained consciousness as he felt a hand unceremoniously searching through his jacket pockets. In his mind the words formed in Portuguese: '*Nâo, nâo sou morto* . . .' His mouth was too dry to articulate, his lips caked with blood. No, in any case, something else should be said. In the darkness he picked up the young Russian's whispered words as he talked to himself without hearing. Elias knew there was nothing in his jacket pockets, the soldiers had taken his papers, his money, his notebook . . . The pen! Tucked away horizontally in an inside pocket, as if in a hiding place. The young prisoner was just flushing it out. Lean pickings. And what's more, he did not know that . . .

'The ink . . . The ink's all dried up . . . But if you could memorize an address . . .'

The Man Who Loved

I

As he witnessed the betrayal of the ideals he had always fought for, his resolve did not falter. In Africa the USSR abandoned bloody remnants of ideals, ruined dreams, the ghosts of those who had believed in them and died from them. I talked to him about this inglorious ending and spoke harshly, as true friends allow themselves to, of his own commitment and the apparent futility of his remaining faithful to it. I was struck by the tone of his reply, that of truths that do not age. In his youth he had learned about the fate of a Russian general, Karbychev, who, as a prisoner of the Nazis, resisted all attempts over long months to turn him, rejecting the most tempting promises, scorning the threats, braving the tortures. On a bitterly cold day the SS made him walk outside naked and began spraying him with a jet of water. The man remained upright, motionless, slowly turning into a statue of ice . . . I remember having suggested to Elias that we were no longer in the same period and that our world was no longer . . . He interrupted me, though not rudely, to remark that he still lived in a world where a woman whose collarbone had been smashed by a soldier's boot could be left to die. 'In your Dostoyevsky,' he added, with a grim smile, 'Ivan rejects the ideal society since creating it would oblige us to witness a child shedding tiny tears. I'm not

*as rigid as that . . . But I am the child who saw his
mother prostitute herself for a mouthful of bread. So,
understand me well, it won't be easy to make a turn-
coat of me . . .'*

I have never written about Elias Almeida's life. I noted
down that fragment a couple of days ago in the plane,
thinking I would read it out at the symposium on
'African Life Stories'. Each participating writer was due
to present a brief personal testimony.

I quickly understood the extent to which I had been
mistaken in my choice of text, so to speak. I had not
been back to Africa for fifteen years . . .

Now at the drinks reception where all the participants are gathered I try to grasp in what way modes
of thought and behaviour have changed. Above all to
grasp what it is that makes those few notes on Elias
completely anachronistic to these people drinking,
smiling at one another, kissing, exchanging cards. At
the centre of the room can be seen a nucleus formed
by the dark suits belonging to the 'fat cat Africans of
the international conference circuit', here to debate
sustainable development. They are protected by a
swirling mass of secretaries and press attachés. Two
cameras from a television crew cut slowly through the
crowd. I can make out the African writer who spoke
this afternoon: in oracular tones he had extolled the
ancestral magic, inaccessible to the European brain,
the traditions and rites without which Africa would no
longer be Africa, palaver trees, the sense of the sacred . . .
He is chatting now to a colleague who, at the same
round-table discussion, made a slashing attack on the

'nostalgia merchants', the 'gravediggers'. All those, in short, who did not believe, like him, that Africa was 'surfing every new wave', 'swinging to the beat of modernity', and even 'grafting its black balls onto the anaemic culture of Europe'. I can also see the lean and frail ('anaemic' . . .) French novelist who, having made two trips to Senegal, claims to be an 'adventurer into darkest Africa'. He is busy going into raptures over a group of traditional singers whose multicoloured flowing robes smack of modern textile manufacture. Next to them a restless circle of rappers who will be performing this evening: smug little gigolo faces, the grimaces of spoilt children of political correctness, wearing outfits that flaunt the ugliness of a domesticated counter-culture, reeking of cash. Finally, beside a score of drawings fixed to the wall, the couple I recognize: the plump white woman with beetroot-coloured hair, one of the conference organizers, and her lover, the artist from Kinshasa. He is giving an interview to the journalists, pointing at his drawings, she watches him a little as if he were her own creation . . .

Is there such a great change, in fact? Over fifteen years, twenty years . . . Then, as now, I could have seen the same thick necks assembled to share out rich pickings. The same intellectuals, capable, like good geisha girls, of dancing to any tune to please the thick necks. A French writer, a self-proclaimed expert in negritude. And how many times before have I not chanced upon couples like this one made up of the plump white woman and her young protégé from Kinshasa.

No, no real change. Quite simply, after fifteen years of forgetting, I had convinced myself that I could one day tell the story of Elias Almeida's life. The passage of time makes fond innocents of us.

Of course some fragments of him will live on in the minds of people who knew him and will say: 'An Angolan committed to a cause long since lost. A courageous man, even absurdly courageous, no doubt loved by women but maintaining an inexplicable attachment to one with whom he had a totally unfulfilled, in point of fact, quite hopeless love affair.' Yes, those who were closest to him could tell that much at best. As for the others (I look round the room), Elias Almeida will never exist for them, they would never want their party to be disrupted by the memory of life stories like his . . . The PA system begins to emit the first bursts of percussion, the guitars utter dull miaowing sounds. The thick necks head for the restaurant. The party can begin.

In my hotel room I have a very physical sense of a life being erased. A few years suffice to transform a living being into this ghost who haunts peoples' memories less and less: a young African who, naively, fought for a better world, loved without success, quietly disappeared. Feverishly I try to remember the details of this obliterated existence, my memory clings to the odd word, the odd gesture . . . But something seen recently encroaches on these echoes of long ago. The previous months, a snatch of a television programme, a discussion on the future of Europe and the voice of a woman very sure of herself, almost scornful: 'You're still living in the fantasy of a France with full employment. But don't forget, globalization has arrived. And if the French don't get back to work, the emerging countries will teach them free market economics . . .' The presenter reminds us of the woman's name: Louise Rimens, the editor of a big financial weekly . . . A *pasionaria* who had 'married the revolution'. Does she remember a young Angolan she talked to tearfully about her blind dog? Cuba, more than thirty years ago . . .

I also recall an article about the scandal of the sale of arms to Angola and the oil quagmire a big French company had been bogged down in. One of the men implicated admitted he had been hampered in his activities by 'an Angolan Robespierre', who opposed all this trafficking very effectively. 'The identity of this upholder of the law,' he wrote, 'remained unknown to me to the very end . . .' Since then the affair has gathered dust in the archives. The company in question has changed its name. The networks have reconstituted themselves. And only a handful of people would still be able to guess that the 'upholder of the law' in question was Elias Almeida.

In fact, he has no other life than this ghostly presence in memories now grown confused, repressed, indecipherable. I remember hastily noting down the stories he told me, joining the dots between our various often chance encounters in Africa, in Europe, in the United States. But I can no longer conceive of any logic that might link these fragments, apart from the failure of all that he dreamed of, the loss of the one he loved.

Out on the terrace, I again locate Lupus, the constellation of the Wolf, in the dense black sky. Down below, on the hotel's broad front steps, the crowd of guests is preparing to go and explore the night life of this African capital. The party goes on. The thick necks settle into grotesque limousines, the rank and file are assigned to clapped-out minibuses. At a certain level of social clownishness, human stupidity almost inspires compassion. On the far side of the frontier, so close to this city, war rages, villages burn, adults kill children, other children become killers. The world against which Elias Almeida fought . . . The door onto the neighbouring terrace opens, two figures hidden in the darkness settle into deckchairs. The fat white woman and her friend from Kinshasa embark on a verbose prelude to coitus.

This evening I decide to abandon the search for any rational order in the fragments of the past my memory has retained. The logic of History, the causes of every war and every peace, universal morality, none of that has ever helped humanity to prevent a boot smashing a woman's collarbone and children learning to kill. It was that night in Lunda Norte that made me wary of all those learned abstractions. Instead of History what I saw then was soldiers gripping a woman crouched on all fours, whom they had just raped and killed. One of them extracting the tiny granules of rough diamonds from her dead mouth. Now a child rigged up in a gas mask thrust his hideous head in at the window of our prison, threatening us with a weapon too heavy for his thin arms. Elias talked to him and learned that the boy's father had been shot by President Neto's regime, which was liquidating 'factionalists'. Uneasily, I clung for a moment to the 'historical logic' of the struggle against the enemies of the revolution. Finally I realized that what this lofty logic came down to was the gaze of that child high on cannabis, Elias's body, covered in infected wounds, and that woman's distorted mouth where a big, breathless, soldier's fingers searched for ugly little pebbles. On his left cheek there was a scar in the form of a star. Next morning he was one of the few to escape the Cuban commandoes . . . I had stopped with Elias close to a pit dug for the raped Zairean woman and the child with his face hidden by a gas mask. The earth was reddish-brown, with a good smell of humid undergrowth. 'The Kremlin will never forgive Neto for renewing contact with Mobutu . . .' Elias murmured as if to himself. Five months later, in September 1979, Neto was dying in Moscow. The logic of History . . . Beside this grave for the Zairean woman and the child the notion of an archaeological dig passed through my mind as in a bad dream: what would the archaeologists of the distant future make of our civilization when they discovered this skeleton of a woman with a few fragments of diamonds in its mouth, and that one of a masked child?

I hasten to write down what I know of Elias Almeida's life. Without imposing any order on these fragments. Sometimes I am tempted by the novelistic play of coincidence: the poet Neto, having become president, kills thousands of men and then dies, as if in a funeral ode, by taking poison in a glass of champagne offered to him by a pretty woman who, quite calmly, watches him die. An easy game, I know, these coincidences. Reality prefers failure, delay, the impossibility of communing in thought with a loved one. When he arrived in the Congo at the age of fifteen to join his father there was an episode Elias had wanted to tell him about: a lorry filled with Portuguese soldiers drives past, a burst of sub-machine gun fire, bullets ripping apart the foliage, birds scatter, others fall and one limps in the dust, its wing broken. The soldiers' laughter, the silence. The grandiose randomness of evil. Above all, Elias wanted to tell his father about the circumstances of his mother's death. 'Yes, I know. I've been told about it,' his father said hurriedly. 'Yes, that's . . . how it is.'

Perhaps the true logic of life might be wholly contained in this unanswerable: 'That's how it is.'

II

Kinshasa. A black and white film.

A fair, milky skin, thick, fleshy thighs: a woman hitches up her tight-fitting skirt and settles herself into a large luxury car. Glaring lights stand out in the night, as always in Africa. The woman's excessively golden hair glitters. Her stiletto heels oblige her to lift her knees quite high as she sits down. Her body folded up on the seat is reminiscent of a . . . yes, a fat turkey trussed for the oven.

In the press of the crowd on the palace staircase I intercept Elias's look, his brief smile. No other exchange should indicate that we are acquainted. With a swift, knowing gaze he points out a face to me, amid the throng of dark suits and evening dresses. An African of about forty, tall, corpulent, a little too tightly squeezed into a designer suit. Dilated eyes, nostrils visibly quivering. He stares at the woman wriggling about on the seat, adjusting her skirt around her broad thighs, as she seeks a comfortable position for her high heels. This feverish attention is lost among the whirlwind of words of farewell, little laughs, grotesque bowings and scrapings, in which 'President' and 'General' are bandied back and forth, the flutter of visiting cards, the bustle of chauffeurs and bodyguards. The man devouring the turkey-woman with his eyes believes he is invisible. On his left cheek I suddenly make out a pale asterisk, the trace of a scar. The face of the soldier retrieving diamonds from the mouth of a dead woman comes back to me. A coincidence? I should like to ask Elias. But he has gone already and, besides, would he know himself?

Several days later I learn that the man with the scar on his cheek is known to our secret services as 'the Candidate'. A Zairean established in Luanda who manages the sale of Angolan oil to the Americans, who have never recognized Marxist Angola. They are thus buying oil from a phantom state! And the 'Marxist' Angolans are buying themselves villas in Europe thanks to the oil sold to the American imperialists with whom they are at war. The logic of History . . . Washington has its money on 'the Candidate' as a probable successor to Mobutu in Zaire. Soviet intelligence have had their eye on this man for several months. The turkey-woman makes a good bait . . .

This frenzied tangle of world affairs, the energy of thousands of men confronting one another, plotting, selling incalculable riches, piling up millions in secret bank accounts, wooing their enemies and tearing their allies to pieces, dragging their countries into long years of war, starving whole regions, paying armies of hacks to glorify their policies, all this crazy global machinery is concentrated that evening in the fleshy body of a blonde woman whom a sweating black man would like to possess.

In Elias's look I perceive better than before the rapid alternation between a fighter's hardness and immense sadness.

A brief while later the dossier on 'the Candidate' is enriched by a filmed sequence: him and the turkey-woman bonded together in a monotonous coupling. From time to time the woman reaches under the man's body to make sure the contraceptive has not slipped . . . There is not much light in the room and, when she gets up, the woman peers at her underclothes to avoid putting them on inside out. From the bed the man watches her doing this, with a stubborn, strangely hostile air. The other, shorter sequence has a greater variety of light and shade. In it the man's half-open mouth can be seen, his eyes slightly bulging, staring at the woman whose head thrusts up and down rhythmically as she fellates him. Then he sleeps, while the woman rummages in a brief-case and, page by page, photographs a thick notebook with glittering gilt edges.

At the year's end comes the greatest surprise of all. Suddenly this whole game becomes completely point-less. The Americans abandon 'the Candidate', having found a creature more suited to their plans. French arms salesmen arrive in the market place and muddy the waters. In Moscow Andropov dies, power slips into an increasingly evident coma. In Luanda one tribe of corrupt men drives out another. The leaders furnish themselves with the services of new networks of traffickers. Bank account numbers are changed. The Angolan President promises the eradication, once and for all, of UNITA, which is supported by the Americans, and the immediate establishment of socialism, assisted by the USSR.

And of all this gigantic farce what remains is Elias Almeida's life, endangered several times, in order (I observe maliciously) to obtain two pieces of film in which a portly African and a buxom white woman can be seen glued together.

What also remains in my memory is Elias's look: cool determination and the sadness of one who no longer has any illusions.

Cabinda. What can be demanded of a life and a death.

Two years later we find ourselves in Cabinda, dining beside the harbour under a sky where the stars mingle with the lights on the oil rigs. Elias has just been spending time in northern Angola 'not far from the forests where those heroic UNITA idiots put us in the lock-up', he says with a smile. His right wrist is in plaster and this shackle, too, is a reminder of that night long ago in Lunda Norte . . . I am on the point of asking him, in the same ironic tones, whether 'the Candidate' could not by any chance be the sergeant who imprisoned us: he had a similar scar on his cheek . . .

A man and a woman, both of them quite elderly, appear in front of the rickety tables on the terrace where we are sitting. They walk one behind the other, joined together by two long planks, which they carry on their shoulders, one on each side of their heads. The resemblance to the wooden collars once used to keep slaves in line immediately comes to mind . . . 'People like them live on a dollar a month,' says Elias softly without looking at me. 'João Alves, that *apparatchik* I knew in Moscow has just bought a second house close to Lisbon. He's delighted that, with the entry into Europe, property prices will go up . . .'

He remains silent for a long while then, still in low tones, talks to me about his mission in Lunda Norte: to smash the diamond barter business, that vital sinew of war for UNITA ('not to mention our "Marxists" in Luanda,' he murmurs with gritted teeth). Arms for diamonds, and with the arms they conquer diamond-bearing territories and can thus buy more arms to conquer further territories. It is the same routine for oil . . .

'So war's a very profitable industry,' he says, nodding towards the oil rigs. 'And what's more, instead of retiring, soldiers get killed, which suits everybody. Nothing new about it as a production cycle. In the old days they stirred up conflicts between tribes to provide themselves with slaves. But slaves were hard work. You had to tie them up, rather like those two old people with their planks, take them to the coast, transport them across the ocean, give them a scrap of food . . . Diamonds can be turned into houses near Lisbon much quicker . . .'

I have an impulse to goad him into the admission I sense maturing within him: why risk his life if the dice are loaded and it is in everyone's interest for this civil war to continue so they grow rich? I do not broach the topic head on, I talk about the videotape of 'the Candidate' and the turkey-woman. This fragment of film implied lengthy approach manoeuvres, attempts at recruitment, blackmail . . . In the vague hope of having 'our man' in a future government. Now all that work had come to nothing, producing only a video reminiscent of a third-rate blue movie . . .

I am expecting a political rationale, a precept I had heard on his lips before now. 'You can't make a revolution in kid gloves.' 'A professional should never ask himself: What's the point? That's a question for Hamlets.' Yes, a half-mocking reply designed to stop all jesuitical moralizing in its tracks.

This time there is no note of irony in his voice. 'You know, maybe it's my age, but I ask less and less of life. I often think it would have been enough for me just to have been able to save that child, you remember, in Lunda Norte, the one who'd put on an old gas mask. That little lad completely high on drink and drugs. I should have told him to hide so as not to be shot in the morning . . .'

The old couple walk back close to the restaurant where we sit at table. Relieved of their burden, the man and woman nevertheless walk as before, one behind the other, with the same heavy tread. Elias watches them walking away, then, without changing his tone, continues: 'And with death it's the same. When I was young I lacked all modesty, I dreamed of it being heroic, flamboyant. On the barricades, in some way or other . . . One day I learned how Antonio Carvalho died, my first master in Marxism. They tortured him appallingly to make him denounce me. Mine was the eye that got in their way, the "man from Moscow" to be got rid of. Carvalho defeated them all because he smiled! Yes. He said nothing, just smiled. Right to the end . . .'

We fell silent, our eyes directed towards the ocean, towards the darkness pock-marked with flares from the oil rigs. By day and night deep in the dense waters, steel tubes suck in the earth's black blood. This oil is transformed into arms, then into the red blood of human beings.

Elias gives a slight shake of his head: 'You say: two scraps of film with that fat pig fucking her . . . It's not as simple as that. Under pressure from the Americans, that fellow had big plans. To create a real Zairean army equipped by the United States. An army of professionals, no longer those gangs of pillagers and drunkards Mobutu has at his disposal. If it had worked we'd have had another war. And we'd have lost it. We managed to sideline that young man with his weakness for beautiful blonde women . . . Another war. Yes. We've already reached seven hundred thousand dead since we started building the radiant future. And those seven hundred thousand include Carvalho. And that child buried with his gas mask on his head . . .'

He is aware of a note of justification in his words, the eternal reasoning of spies: devious manoeuvres, this necessary evil in order to prevent a much greater evil. Yes, the ousting of one crook to save thousands of innocents . . . The old argument revolutionaries and other benefactors of humanity generally put forward. We exchange glances, aware of what can lie hidden behind this 'necessary evil'.

Elias begins to talk with a more relaxed, almost amused, air: 'It's true that Zairean looked very like the sergeant who interrogated us at Lunda Norte. That scar from a bullet in the shape of an asterisk. But it wasn't him. Just a man of the same type. An ambitious career soldier thrust towards the top either by ourselves or by the Westerners. One of those pawns they try to turn into a leader. Sometimes they crack. Sometimes they succeed: and you get Bokassa, Idi Amin, Mengistu and the rest. If you can call that success. Yes, the same mould. The ingredients are always similar: money, an almost sensual desire for power, the flesh of women. I've met humans in this mould in Guinea-Bissau, in Brazzaville . . . To begin with you actually think you're meeting the same person. And it's not so much their physique that's deceptive. There are big ones and little ones. No, it's . . . their eyes, which seem to be saying: I'm ready for anything. Like that Zairean you saw. To ride in the limousine with that fat blonde he was ready to cover a whole country in graves.'

We walk to the end of a jetty where we can feel the keen nocturnal force of the wind off the open sea. Elias's shirt flaps around his body, making him look thinner, more fragile. In my mind's eye I have a sudden vision of him, alone, assailed by a crowd of men whose faces are impossible to make out, they look so alike. Men cast in that mould, I tell myself, against whom he strives to fight . . . It is a losing battle and he knows it. History, whose course he dreamed of changing is, in fact, nothing more than an elegant metaphor and a man staring at a woman's broad thighs as she sits on a car seat, yes, often the hungriness of such a stare counts for more in this metaphor than the noblest of ideals and the commitments to causes made by heroes.

Beneath our feet, in the marine depths, the steel tubes continue to pump the black blood that will turn into money, arms, the red blood of the dead, bought female flesh. I want to say this to Elias, to shake his faith, to mock his obstinacy. Two months previously I had seen Anna at a reception at the Soviet embassy in Maputo, where her husband had been posted. She reminded me of a big smiling doll, uttering bland inanities, batting her eyelashes with the regularity of an automaton. I was positioned somewhat to one side and I could see that the fingers of her left hand were kneading the handle of her handbag, her thumbnail was tearing the leather and this tensed hand was the only true and living part of this clockwork doll.

'Two months ago, at Maputo,' I say, 'I ran into . . . Anna.'

Maputo. Beyond words.

I take a breath before deciding to tell him what I think of this woman, what a Russian can think of this Russian woman, and what might perhaps be missed by an African or, quite simply, the man who loved her and still loves her. I don't have time to go on. Elias starts to talk very softly, his gaze lost in the supple motion of the waves slipping along the jetty. An evening, the same gathering of guests in an embassy garden, the same expressions, either rigid or, on the contrary, animated by the grimaces of social chit-chat, the same routine conversations where no one listens to anyone. He is separated from Anna by a few feet of this air laden with hypocrisy. They cannot speak to one another, they must not betray their past in any way, not a gesture, not a smile. For them to stand so close to one another without recognizing one another is the best way of pretending to be strangers. She looks like a big, beautiful doll, he thinks, and doubtless everyone else thinks the same. He has aged, she must be telling herself, his hair is turning grey, there's that scar on his temple and his wrist in the plaster cast concealed by the sleeve of his shirt. She lets this doll do the talking for her, he thinks, and is becoming just as I knew her in Moscow, that quivering of the eyelashes is exactly as it used to be . . . For several minutes, as the guests come and go across the garden, they are left alone. Without turning his head towards Anna, Elias recites the names of streets in Moscow at random. She repeats them, in a hesitant echo, then grows bolder and murmurs: 'So you haven't forgotten them . . .' Other names, precious passwords, are whispered: those of little stations far away in the middle of the *taiga*. The beautiful doll smiles at a couple who greet her in passing. Anna whispers again, her lips hardly open: 'I've had a letter from Sarma. They're asking when you'll come back . . . *So glad to meet you . . . Oh, very lovely! Especially Maputo game reserve and Inhaca Island . . .*' The doll speaks to a couple, an extremely suntanned man, a pale, sickly-looking woman. Elias moves away, carrying with him just the melody of that 'when you'll come back . . .'

That night in Cabinda I believe I have understood what he truly experienced at Sarma: a life that comes into being when History, having exhausted its atrocities and promises, leaves us naked beneath the sky, confronting only the gaze of the one we love.

Some weeks after that encounter with Anna at the reception he almost died in an ambush to the north of Moxico. He hardly mentioned it to me, not wanting to strike a warrior's pose. All I remember is the comment he made softly, as if to himself: 'When death stares us coolly in the eye we perceive that in our lives there have been a few hours, of sunlight or of darkness, a few faces to which we return continually, and that what has kept us alive, in fact, is the simple hope of finding them again . . .'

Moxico. Games for grown-ups.

For us, the years that will follow are to be a time of defeat, flight, scattering. Elias will live through them without any change of attitude, as if the goal he has always pursued had not lost all meaning. One day I will learn that he has conducted negotiations single-handed with the men of UNITA in southern Moxico and succeeded in avoiding the resumption of fighting. Just on that occasion, just in that area, saving the lives of the inhabitants of just one village. I will remember what he said about the modesty of the tasks he hence-forth set himself. In the conflagration Africa was entering into at that time this modest success will seem to me more important than all the planning for the planet. Throughout the discussions in a hut in the village a child was playing at the other end of the room; sitting on the ground, she was building a pyramid, made up of empty cartridge cases from a machine gun, on top of a wobbly table. When the argument was at its height and Elias no longer had any hope of reaching agree-ment and therefore, of remaining alive once the bargaining broke down, the whole edifice of cartridge cases collapsed with a metallic clatter. The grown-ups looked round. The child froze, contrite. Elias remem-bered that village in Kivu half burned in the war and a little girl curled up between the legs of a low table, the child trembling so much that the piece of furniture seemed alive . . . He began talking again with the arrogant strength of one no longer concerned about his own survival. This indifference in the face of death, as he already knew, gives one a great advantage over those who have yet to come to terms with their fear of dying.

Brazzaville. The purity of gemstones.

He was on his way out of his hotel when two policemen in civilian clothes accosted him. Everything now happened with split-second timing. He looked them up and down scornfully, handed one of them his suitcase and, without raising his voice, ordered: 'Here. Put this in my car out there. A grey Mercedes . . .' The trick worked perfectly. The tone of calm, peremptory authority. The policemen, who were supposed to be arresting him, obeyed, walked over to the exit, subjugated, hypnotized, and it was only once outside, where no 'grey Mercedes' was to be seen, that they roused themselves and retraced their steps at the double. Elias had time to slip out through the side entrance, in front of which a car was waiting for him . . .

From those final years I retain a handful of such anecdotes that he used to recount to me with a smile when we ran into one another between flights, in the course of some mission or other. The memory of them is buried in a jumble of details that seem utterly pointless today but which were a matter of life and death at the time. The business with the suitcase . . . It is a routine technique, in fact, known as the 'relay-object', which he had doubtless learned during the course of his training as an intelligence agent. The procedure is simple: if

anyone obstructs you, you must on any pretext whatever hand them an object which encumbers them and
for which they become responsible. To a fierce gate-
keeper barring your way at the entrance to a protected
place you hand a briefcase, remarking: 'General X's
sergeant will come to collect this at 6.30 hours. Take
good care of it.' And while the guard is pondering, overwhelmed by the weight of the onus put on him, you
pass through.

What remains in my memory is Elias's smile as he
told me about these tricks of the trade, sometimes
adding: 'So in the end our practical training in Moscow
wasn't wasted. All those assaults on the "presidential
palace" . . . And by and large, I can confirm, it does
happen more or less the way our instructors taught us
it would. And the hardest thing of all is to avoid killing
the children when there are bursts of gunfire on all
sides . . . In our training they were celluloid dolls.'

Behind his light touch with the detail lay concealed
long wars, sometimes raging, sometimes running out of
steam, villages populated with corpses and one morning,
a fine spring morning, that youth dragging his mother's
body, riddled with bullet wounds, along a road in the
south of Moxico. Elias took them to the nearest town.
The intolerable weight of that body.

Behind the anecdote about the policemen encumbered by
a 'relay-suitcase' there had been very discreet negotiations that evening in Brazzaville between the emissaries
of the South African regime (the demons of apartheid!)
and the representatives of the socialist regime of Angola.
The caution of two reptiles feeling one another in the

dark, sniffing one another, hesitating between confrontation and doing a deal. And all mixed up with this nest
of vipers, several CIA agents, as well as those of UNITA,
and the indiscreet oilmen from Elf and the diamond buyers
(that Lebanese of Armenian origin, among others, the lid
of his left eye grotesquely distended by a magnifying
glass) and the arms salesmen, one of whom remarked
to me one day with cheerful amazement: 'I've sold such
a lot, there really shouldn't be many people left on
earth . . .'

Some years later the diamond merchant would be
discovered at his desk with his bloodied head resting on
a pile of gemstones. The wife of the president who offered
his hospitality for the secret meeting at Brazzaville would
be accused of this murder. The arms salesmen would
change the names of their agencies and the oilmen those
of their companies. UNITA would be decapitated. But
this would make no difference to the background noise
at those African summits: the discreet chink of diamonds
being appraised, the pumping of black blood beneath
the waves, the crunch of armoured vehicles on the rutted
tarmac of cities in flames, the screams of raped women,
children having their throats cut, the crackle of the flames
on the burning roofs of huts, and somewhere at some
great film festival the ecstatic whispers surrounding a
star who is wearing around her neck stones of the first
water, so rare, so pure . . .

At the emperor's. Twelve pianists.

Yet another detail strangely preserved from oblivion: it
could be called a dumb show, for the performance was

entirely silent and the recounting of it left us speech-
less, giving rise to an almost metaphysical amazement.
One of Bokassa's residences, a room where the lights
are low, a dozen piano stools in a row occupied by
naked women who have their backs turned. A handclap and in a perfectly synchronized movement all twelve
of them swivel round to face the master. Who has a
strangely weary, almost aggrieved air, as if this carnal
treasure disappointed him profoundly . . . The vision of
these 'beautiful pianists with no piano', as Elias called
them, was on a level with other acts of depravity
dreamed up by the tyrants of that continent, the
pharaonic cathedrals and castles erected upon the graves
of famine victims. But the twelve piano stools went
further, for this spinning harem touched the most sensi-
tive spot in a man's heart: the impossibility of loving,
even while possessing, so much flesh, purchased in
Africa, in Europe and elsewhere . . . The master of the
pianists – the 'Emperor'! – would be overthrown a year
later in a country strewn with mutilated bodies. And
amid all the jumble of wealth and obscenities that such
a reign leaves in its wake, we are left with the picture
of those twelve piano stools, absurdly lined up in a hall
hung with valuable pelts.

Moscow. The death of a poet.

That vignette would soon find its echo during the trip
to Moscow on which Elias accompanied President
Agostinho Neto. The poison that killed the President
had the characteristic of causing a spasm in the cardiac
muscle which made the death appear to be a perfectly

convincing heart attack. It took just a psychological trigger, an additional rush of blood, to unleash the effect of the substance . . . The President was entering the suite placed at his disposal when, in a small circular room he was passing through, this woman (she was busy cleaning the keyboard of a grand piano: a discordant lament of merry notes) greeted him and informed him that she would be taking care of his nocturnal requirements. The sentence was uttered in correct but somewhat rudimentary Portuguese, allowing for some ambiguity: nocturnal requirements? . . . A young blonde woman, an apron fitting tightly over broad hips, emphasizing a slender waist . . . She stared at him as if awaiting a reply. He hesitated, sat down in an armchair, smiled at her. She settled down on the piano stool, as if she were resting for a moment before resuming her dusting. Beside the armchair, on a low table, stood several bottles of drink . . . Did he succumb straight away? After a glass? After an embrace? Or did they have time to undress and he to take his pleasure? The next day the Soviet authorities announced that the Angolan President, suffering from a serious illness, had come to the USSR to be treated but, despite all the efforts of the best doctors, he had not survived.

Elias will retain from all this the piano stool he had seen the previous day when he brought a dispatch to the President's secretary. A quite ordinary, black stool, like the ones the Central African tyrant's 'pianists' had spun round on. Details, yes, but it was perhaps the first time that he perceived with such intensity the supreme absurdity that ruled the lives and deaths of human beings. Before they left, the Soviets showed the members of the Angolan delegation a short documentary film. It was an account of the conflict between perfidious Somalia and faithful Ethiopia. Panoramic shots displayed the titanic disembarking of hundreds of armoured vehicles, entire squadrons, countless artillery pieces. A complete prepackaged war, handed on a plate by the Empire to its Ethiopian protégé. And then the results: arid stretches of the Ogaden in Ethiopia, covered in Somalian corpses and the debris of their weapons. At its close, the camera, no doubt mounted on a helicopter, swooped down over endless columns of distraught prisoners . . . The film had no soundtrack and this silence gave the images an even more crushing force, a bleak and categorical argument. It was a lesson, yes. The Angolan leaders were supposed to appreciate the weight of the vengeance that fell upon the enemies of the Empire.

Moscow. An hour with Anna.

Elias had an extremely brief meeting with Anna, on the very last evening of that visit to Moscow. Agostinho Neto's body, the entrails cleaned of all trace of poison, had already been prepared to be sent back to Luanda. In subdued tones the members of the delegation, some devastated, some relieved, were discussing the film they had just seen. Elias managed to escape, rang up from a public phone box, learned that Anna was celebrating her husband Vadim's birthday with friends. She went down into the park where Elias was waiting for her and they began walking under the mild September rain by a light reminiscent of the soft blue haze of a spring

they had never lived through together. At first sight
Anna's face seemed to him coarsened by a fixed smile
intended for her guests, by smooth, impersonal make-
up. Little by little the showers banished this fixity from
her features, and he saw, perhaps only with the vision
that lay hidden in his heart, the young woman who
once used to lead him through the snow-covered streets
of Moscow. The one who believed in a knight brave
enough to go down into the arena and bring back a
glove for his fair lady. The one who boarded the train
with the scent of a forest in winter clinging to the grey
wool of her dress . . . They hardly spoke and before
parting (she had to hurry back to rejoin the guests,
doubtless already uneasy about her absence), they
embraced with such violence that he slightly grazed his
lip in this clumsy and feverish kiss.

The Logic of History.

I know they saw one another again in Africa on several
occasions, even during the years when the USSR's im-
perial adventure on the black continent was drawing
to a close. Lucapa, Kinshasa, Maputo, Mogadishu . . .
Elias spoke little of them to me and it was especially
those few days spent in Moscow at the time of Neto's
death that he sought to describe to me, as if they offered
a digest of all the contradictions of his life as a fighter.
He told me things he did not have time to recount to
Anna, and in any case would never have told her.
Details that suddenly offered proof of the madness of
History. Yes, piano stools and a dozen whores trained
to spin round on them at a handclap. And that stool

where a young woman sits before supervising a man's death agony with professional calm. And beyond the farcical insanity of these coincidences, millions of men pitched against one another in the name of a hatred that will appear stupid the next day, after these men have been bled to death. So then another hatred will have to be invented and dressed up in humanistic or messianic rags, placated with the sound of tank tracks on the tarmac of ruined cities, with the roar of big guns firing on unarmed men. And all of this so that in a great hall where the walls are hung with pelts, a man, weary of massacres, wealth and female flesh, should rest his heavy and nauseated gaze on the backsides of women as they spin round on their piano stools. And so that another man, an occasional poet, should suddenly let his glass of brandy slip onto the carpet and tumble out of his armchair, his eyes rolling upwards, at the feet of a woman whose breasts he has just been fondling. The circle is complete. History has done its work.

There are a few loose ends, of no use to the specialists who will be writing it: that diamond merchant, his face crushed into a glittering mound of gemstones and, in a documentary film about the war between Ethiopia and Somalia, a sequence that probably passed unnoticed by the makers, a goat wounded by shrapnel thrashing about around its stake as the columns of victorious armoured vehicles surge past.

All he had to counter the insanity of this farce, in truth, was his love.

London. Postscript to History.

I saw him again in London, scarcely two years before
the disappearance of the USSR, before the 'end of
History', as proclaimed by a Japanese visionary, whom
everyone took seriously at the time. It was the honey-
moon between Russia and the West, a great 'phew!' of
relief at the grinning softness of the Empire which, with
Gorbachev, was learning to smile and calling this
'democracy'. For the first time, perhaps, I perceived in
Elias's words the sarcasm of a man betrayed. 'You'll
see,' he had said. 'You're going to become best friends
with the USA, ultra-obedient students of capitalism.
When the USSR no longer exists . . .'

Such remarks seemed preposterous at the time. The
Empire had lost none of its power and was capable, as
some years previously, of waging several wars at once,
in Afghanistan, in Ethiopia, in Angola . . . Unwilling to
contradict him for fear of upsetting the one within him
whose life had been lived in the name of a dream, I
adopted the somewhat condescending tone (I now
realize) that the crushing weight of our country permitted
when we addressed our allies, the 'auxiliaries' of the
USSR's messianic project. Half seriously and half in jest
I remarked that you can't make a revolution 'in kid
gloves' and that History, as Lenin said, 'is not the pavement on the Nevsky Prospekt' . . . I had heard these
maxims, tossed out like epigrams, from Elias's own lips.

He seemed not to have heard me, his gaze suddenly
fixed on what no one apart from himself could see. His
voice became very calm, detached. 'For such a dream
of fraternity to succeed there would have to be people

like Karbychev. Yes, there would have to be a faith that drives out the little buzzing insect within us, that little fly, the fear of dying. But, above all, we should have to know how to love. Just simply, to love. Then it would be unthinkable for a woman thrown to the ground to have her collarbone smashed with the kick of a boot . . .'

I now remember clearly how on that night in London he told me about General Karbychev, the prisoner transformed by the Nazis into an ice statue. And I sensed then, as never before, the extent to which Elias was alone, as alone as a man upright beneath lashing cascades of water as they turn him into a block of ice.

What I had taken for a fanciful prophecy came to pass soon afterwards: the Empire closed down the war in Afghanistan, was beaten hollow at Mavinga in southern Angola, prepared pathetically to abandon Ethiopia . . . I ran into Elias in Luanda just after the defeat at Mavinga, where the Soviet instructors turned out to be such hopeless strategists. He was emerging from a hospital where he had been treated for a number of wounds on the arms and face. I was expecting some reference to his disagreement with the battle plan, the tactical intelligence the commanders had ignored . . . I imagined a bitter but also grievously triumphant tone, the attitude of one who had got it right and had not been listened to. None of that. He tightened the strip of bandages around his head, smiled at me: 'I have the feeling they're going to send us all to the Horn of Africa soon. Closer to the happier Arab lands. Look, I've got my Lawrence of Arabia headdress on already. The war no longer makes any sense, you know. There are people fighting on both sides only interested in filling their own pockets. And, if they're lucky, one day having a dozen naked pianists on piano stools of their own. Ring down the curtain!'

When I found myself on Somali soil some months later I did not even remember that prophetic joke. We no longer had time to recall the past: the hell of Mogadishu engulfed us in the violent and routine madness of fighting, in the recurring faces of the dead, among which only those of children could still shock us.

III

Before arriving in Mogadishu Elias had spent a week in Moscow, where he had seen Anna once more. He told me this in a couple of words on the telephone, just before I set off for Somalia myself. In the plane I imagined what their encounter might have been like, a Sunday in winter in a big Moscow apartment filled with objets d'art accumulated during the couple's tours abroad. As a result of working in Africa, Vadim must certainly have covered the walls in fantastic masks, spears whose shafts are decorated with bunches of sisal, shields of hippopotamus skin. And an array of figurines, mascots and charms on every ledge. 'Now they'll be able to add some of those curved daggers with jigsaw sheaths to them,' I said to myself, 'the kind you get in the Horn of Africa . . .', visualizing this oppressive apartment with its thick carpets and massive furniture. Vadim had been working in the Yemen. Then, after the start of the civil war there and the flight of the Soviets, they had sent him to Somalia. Anna had returned to Moscow to help their son, who was embarking on his university studies. She would soon be going to join her husband.

I believed I could not be much mistaken in picturing her with the features of a woman of forty, still beautiful, with a figure that had become more ample, more imposing. In other words, the solid wife of an *apparatchik*, intelligent and self-confident, aware of her success and of the exceptional comfort of this apartment where one winter's day, without any special emotion, she awaited the visit of an Angolan friend, yes, an old friend from twenty years ago.

I pictured her thus, beautiful, calm, walking slowly through the rooms, adjusting a picture here, a mask there. And this calmness seemed to me to be the most grievous defeat to all that Elias had dreamed of.

Our plane, an army aircraft, had headed for Addis Ababa, from where some of us were due to fly on to Mogadishu. During these long flights I was accustomed to hearing animated debates among the soldiers, each one holding forth about 'his' war in this or that country in the world. This time the dark cabin remained quiet. And when the occasional conversation developed, all it amounted to was mere scraps of voices, worn out with weariness and a shared awareness: it was time to pull out of all these quagmires of the 'anti-imperialist struggle'.

My neighbour was not even taking part in these terse exchanges, he was dozing, his ears blocked by the headphones of his tape recorder. His was an odd head: a very young face (he could hardly have been more than thirty) and completely white hair, that bluish, fragile white that very old men have. In the susurration of his headphones I identified a number of pieces following one another without any musical logic: the breathlessly tremulous 'Petites Fleurs', followed, who knows why, by Tchaikovsky's 'Valse Sentimentale', which was encroached on by the breathy trilling of 'Summertime' and suddenly, after a screech that betrayed a recording from a disc, a classical fragment of wistful beauty, mingling violins and organ . . . I heard only the first few bars of it. My neighbour began twisting in his seat, rubbing his brow. By the glow of a small light, I could see his eyes glistening. His tape recorder was an old model and at intervals the little cassette jammed. As it had now, since he had to take it out and adjust the tape by turning the spool with his finger. Incredulously, I saw that he was laughing softly and that his eyes were brimming with tears . . . He noticed my astonished glance, took off his headphones. 'As soon as I stop the music I want to howl . . .' Not knowing how to respond to this admission, I gave a slight cough and murmured: 'I see . . . Yes. It's true. Music can . . .' But he was already talking, his eyes half closed, in the grip of a past that would not let him go. As an army doctor, he had been sent to Afghanistan at the age of twenty-six, quickly got used to restoring bodies riddled with shrapnel, repairing lacerated limbs. Without any particular qualms, thanks to the indifference learned during his years as a medical student. Until that day, in the Baghlan mountains: a convoy of lorries with a tank at its head, children at the roadside laughing and waving their arms as the vehicles drove past. Invited on board by the tank crew, he is crammed into the smoke-filled turret where he can feel the force of this roaring mass of steel trans-mitted to his body, one that smashes through every obstacle with its tracks. This power has the effect of a fierce intoxication. He asks the driver for a light, the latter turns his head, offers him his lighter. The vehicle swerves off the road slightly, returns to it at once but it is already too late. There is a grinding of brakes and everything is mixed up: cold air rushing into the turret, the blinding sun, the shrill cries of the villagers, the cursing of the soldiers jumping to the ground . . . Then, despite all those sounds, silence falls. On the tank's tracks and under its tracks, a child's body, crushed, hacked to pieces . . .

In cases like this, he knows, some people start drinking or take refuge behind extra boorishness and cynicism, or else forget, or kill themselves. From now on he becomes a prey to these frequent attacks of weeping, a ridiculous reaction that prevents him doing his work. The solution he has found is this old tape recorder which murmurs softly in a corner of the operating theatre and which, in the end, everyone gets used to . . .

I learn that he is called Leonid, that he comes from Leningrad, that his grandfather had been a doctor and died during the siege. So it was destiny, or an utterly stupid mischance, that took that young man to an Afghan village where he had an impulse to smoke . . .

He, too, is going to Mogadishu. 'Mind you, given the situation there,' he concludes, 'I think we'll be taking off again pretty quickly . . .' and he puts his headphones back on again.

Destiny . . . Behind each of the shadowy figures crammed into that plane there is doubtless a story something like that day of sunshine in the Baghlan mountains, the lorries, the soldiers grinning at the children, then the shouting, the blood . . .

I once more picture a pretty woman of forty, a kind of Soviet bourgeoise, seated in the middle of a drawing room overloaded with rare and precious objects, a woman waiting for an African, yes, a black man foolish enough to have loved her for twenty years, a man grown old, who has just had several stitches removed from his arm and above his left cheekbone.

And then one evening, in a street in the Somalian capital ravaged by gunfire, I have an opportunity to talk with Elias at length. The very last opportunity. I am not aware of this at the time and am more concerned about the progress of the fighters, who are loosing off machine guns in all directions as they advance towards the fortress-villa of the presidential palace. The house where we are hiding has been ransacked and half burned and is therefore no longer interesting, which makes it safe. Even the electric cables have been ripped out, as well as the skirting boards, the hinges from the doors and beneath the window there, I can see it now, some of the bricks are already loose. The whole of Mogadishu seems to have been eviscerated, scoured right down to its mineral shell. On the doorstep of our hiding place lies an open refrigerator, doubtless abandoned by those who fled the shooting. The wrapping on a large pack of milk shows the use-by date: a surrealist piece of information, the milk is good until tomorrow . . .

We have just been taking part in long and fruitless negotiations with the members of *Manifesto,* one of the innumerable opposition forces locked in combat with the very weak 'strong man' of the regime, President Syad Barré, once a friend of the USSR, then its enemy, and now an old man shut away within the fortress of the Villa Somalia. His opponents have already formed themselves into a government and, while making speeches about the future of the country, these gentlemen are squabbling over the ministerial portfolios they count on obtaining after the overthrow of Barré. They are ready to form alliances with anyone at all, the USSR, America, the devil. In fact with whoever will supply the most arms and money in the shortest possible time. They are hesitant and lack ruthlessness. One cannot count on them. Soon the real warlords will arrive, who will have none of their reservations. Furthermore, it is clear that the Moscow analysts have as poor an understanding of this country as the American strategists. But the salient point is that there is less and less for the experts in history to understand. For this city's only history is mere survival, the phases of it are recorded in corpses: these two bodies, among others, a few yards from our refuge, two youths, probably the ones who had to abandon the fridge and run, and fell beneath a burst of gunfire. And the chronology of this History gone mad is documented in the use-by date on a pack of milk swollen by the heat.

We are waiting for nightfall to be able to leave the area. The fighters will be active for another half hour, shooting, killing, stocking up their reserves of food. Then they will go back to their quarters, as they do every day, to lose themselves, some in the thirst-provoking nirvana of khat, some in the caresses of a female companion in arms. The city, dark, without water, without links to the outside world, will become a dot in space amid the stars.

The woman Elias begins to talk about is not at all like the present-day Anna I had imagined through my half-slumber in the plane. Instead, she is thinner and weary, and when she stands against the light beside the window her pale face blends with the silvery swirling of the snowflakes outside the glass. At first, like a clockwork toy animated by the last few turns of the key, she played the part of a worldly Muscovite woman, a diplomat's wife showing a friend round her luxurious apartment. But within a few minutes the clockwork runs down, comes to a standstill. 'There came a time when we'd had enough of all those African bits and pieces. Besides, it's better like this. With all the masks they make for the tourists, there soon won't be any forests left . . .' The clockwork within her comes to life in one last spasm, just to say that, unlike other diplomat's wives, she has a job and that at the embassy they have entrusted her with work on data processing . . . They smile at one another, aware of the futility of the roles they are trying to play: she, a modern woman who has achieved a brilliant international career; he, a champion of human rights who braves all dangers (in the falseness of those first few minutes he had spoken briefly about the battle at Mavinga, where he was wounded. What an idiot!).

They fall silent, observe the fluttering of white above the bare trees in the courtyard. He is aware of the slenderness of Anna's hand in his own. She begins speaking without turning her head towards him.

'I've lived a life . . . in fact, I constructed it, this life . . . which I should not have lived. And yet, you see, I feel I absolutely had to live through it, such as it was, this life, to be capable of denying it. A lot of people can probably judge their lives like this. But the difference is that you and I love one another . . .'

The snow tumbles even more heavily out of the

darkening air. Elias draws a breath, preparing to reply, but suddenly a toy standing on the television set comes to life: a plastic crocodile that opens its jaws, moves its feet and emits a growl with a jazzy tune. 'It's my son's clock. That means it's time for the television news . . .' They both laugh softly and wait for the reptile to finish its performance. Anna goes on talking, but in a voice as if liberated, less cautious.

'You told me one day that the world must be changed. Because it was intolerable for a soldier to smash a woman's collarbone with a kick of his boot. But you haven't really succeeded in changing it, this world . . .'

'I'd have hated myself if I hadn't fought to do so . . .'

'If you'd married me you wouldn't have had time to fight, admit it.'

'Even yesterday I should have replied: wrong, of course I would! But I don't want to lie any more. If I'd married you I'd have become a fat Angolan *apparatchik* who'd spend his time opening accounts in the West and counting everything in barrels and carats . . . And I'd have looked like . . . Yes, that crocodile. But less fun.'

She seems not to have heard his joking remark.

'In the end this was the thought that kept me alive. I said to myself: very well, I'm living with a man I don't love. The years go by and it will always be like this. Till I die. And then I remembered that woman they laid on the ground in front of her child and the child sees his mother's collarbone is broken . . . And then I said to myself that the only way to love you was to let you fight against that world. I suffered a lot but I believed I was doing the right thing. And now it's too late. We can't go back any more . . .'

They do not switch on the lights and in the darkness Elias can see Anna's eyes, her gaze lost in an invisible procession of days, suns, moments.

'But what if we tried to go back?' It is suddenly hard for him to control his voice, although it is finally saying precisely what he wanted to say. An improbable but unbelievably real, true and vital dream. He tries to make it less abrupt, to find a justification, an excuse for it. 'You know, Anna, to tell you the truth, I shall soon have very little choice. There won't be much of a future for the person I've been all this time. Your country no longer needs me. Mine, governed as it is, will do everything in its power to make me disappear. So I'll be forced to go back. I thought we could do it together . . .'

'Go back . . . But go back where?'

'Back to Sarma.'

He leaves her at nightfall. The streets are already almost empty, the same streets, he thinks, as twenty years ago, the same slow swirling of the snow . . .

A few dozen yards from his hotel three men suddenly block his path. Young, dressed in leather jackets. Heavy, wary faces. Elias steps aside slightly, feels his muscles tense ready for a fight. In a flash all the disgust for these Moscow brawls floods in: the collective beating up of a dirty negro. Except that now, facing these three cretins in their leather gear, there stands a body covered in scars, raked by bullets . . . He clenches his fists, lowers his chin . . . '*Excuse me. Can you change this for a few dollars?*' Their English accents are comical and indeed the whole performance makes their faces look singularly foolish. All three of them look like recalcitrant pupils taking an oral exam. '*No dollars,*' he replies, '*just Mongolian tugriks!*' He smiles, walks round the trio, who are lost in confusion over how to translate his reply. On arriving at the hotel, he goes to the bar and orders a drink.

In this country '*A few dollars*' has replaced the urge to smash a black person's face in. The progress is undeniable. He drinks, shuts his eyes. Deep within him these words that no longer belong to anyone resonate on their own in their fragile truth: 'To go back . . . Back to Sarma . . .'

The days that followed our conversation in the burned-out house were filled with bombardments and gunfire, the panic of foreigners fleeing the city, the rage or despair of the Somalis staying behind there, often to be killed. I did not see Elias again nor did I have time to think again about his words. Once only, in a brief grievous insight, I perceived that his love for Anna, their love, resembled that great gulf of the sky on the night we had spoken together for the last time. A superbly starry sky above a city that was getting ready to die. Like that black chasm, their love needed no words, too remote from the lives of human beings. Within myself I could feel a wariness, a doubt, the need for proof.

And yet I sensed that belief in this love was the ultimate belief of my own life, the faith beyond which nothing here on earth would have made sense any longer.

From the threshold of our shelter we had followed the shuffling of furtive footfalls in the street, shadows slipping along. Elias tilted his head back and murmured: 'Do you remember the sky in Lunda Norte? Hold on, I'm going to find the constellation of the Wolf . . .'

IV

A whole lifetime separates me from that night in Somalia. Mogadishu in ruins, a capital which, with obstinacy, almost with relish, was committing suicide day by day. And now, at the other end of Africa, in a quite different Africa, the tranquil streets of Conakry, this big hotel facing the sea, the nauseating feeling of being a rich tourist in the tropics.

I see a constellation in the night sky as I move away from the glaring lights of the People's Palace. A few seconds suffice for the realization to dawn that every one of our actions occurs beneath the giddy remoteness of these stars. And yet we do everything possible to forget this boundless judgement, to be judged only by ourselves. Long ago, in a city strewn with corpses, a man who was perhaps my only true friend and who had only a few days left to live pointed out the constellation of the Wolf to me and reminded me that we had already seen it on the night of our first meeting in the forests of northern Angola, that night when, still very young, I was so afraid to die . . . It was enough to let one's gaze wander among these stars for the fear to begin to weaken and for death to seem temporary, provisional. Like our lives . . .

I hear footsteps on the gravel of the path that surrounds the Palace. The young woman who is guiding our group of writers runs up to me and summons me to come quickly and take my place at the round-table discussion on 'African Life Stories in Literature'.

The debate is already under way. For the first few moments I listen to it as if it were in an unknown language. In memory I am still at the side of the man who has only a few days to live as he gazes at the sky above the ruins of Mogadishu.

Little by little the meaning of what is being said becomes clear to me. Two viewpoints confront one another: the 'afro-pessimists' and the 'afro-optimists'. The latter are drawn from the ranks of the Africans comfortably settled in the West, globalized blacks, to some extent. The 'pessimists' speak of colonization, slavery, negritude. The 'optimists' give half-smiles as they listen to them. They call for self-projection into the future, a balanced perspective on the black man's burden, a reaching out beyond the historic divides between civilizations. The 'traditionalists'' pitch is the inexpiable guilt of the whites, the ancestral wisdom of the African . . . The card played by the 'moderns' is a matter-of-fact view of the colonial past, the new Africa, the continent, in the words of one of them, 'bubbling with vitality and with the libido of a geyser'. The public salutes him with a burst of applause and even several shouts of 'yeah!'.

In the hall at the end of the front row I recognize the organizer with beetroot-coloured hair, my neighbour at the hotel. She sits next to her friend, the Congolese artist. From time to time she consults her watch, then exchanges a little grimace of complicity with the young man, which means: 'Once this palaver's over, we're off.'

Yes, a palaver, she's not wrong. French is the language of the colonizer, complain the 'traditionalists', the white man's weapon that has reduced African cultures to silence. The 'moderns' retort: no, French is our trophy, our spoils of war. We can do with it what we like. French has violated our African mentality. No, anorexic French is being regenerated by an insemination of negritude. This turn of phrase comes from the Togolese writer who has just been talking about 'the libido of a geyser'. It scores a bull's-eye. A guffaw of approval ripples through the hall. The line of dark suits in the front row, occupied by the 'fat cats of the international conference circuit', stirs. Hissing chuckles can be heard from them. During the morning these men have concluded their important cogitations on sustainable development in Africa and now they are relaxing as they listen to the ranting of the novelists, who are simply 'geisha girls', performing a few choice routines for them. Encouraged by the example of the Togolese writer, the participants in the discussion set about demonstrating Africa's fecundating powers. Anything goes: animist priests, whose magic enhances men's sexual performance; women's exuberant beauty ('breasts, two great gourds filled with milk and honey', one of the writers quotes himself); a cunning husband's skill at provoking the rivalry between his wives. I learn that in one African country the men call their mistresses 'offices' and that in Congolese villages the daughter to be married off is nicknamed 'the little dog'. The audience laughs, the novelists vie with one another. Repudiated wives, husbands betrayed with an uncle, a father, a brother, a son . . . Penises 'like a bamboo stem', sweat 'trickling in rivulets between the shoulder blades and streaming into the groove between her buttocks as her lover grips them' . . . All this accompanied by talk of sorcerers, eclipses of the sun, dances and trances.

Tales of men and women and yet at no time, I tell myself in perplexity, does love appear, plain love, with its insane generosity, its spirit of self-sacrifice. Here the talk is of prenuptial bargaining, long marriage rituals, and a whole commerce of paid-for couplings and bride prices, even virginity being rewarded with a goat . . .

A memory comes back to me, the tale of a man tortured with the strappado, deprived of food and water, who told me he would have accepted that suffering all over again in order to find himself for a moment beside the woman he loved.

The notion of talking about him here, in this hall, suddenly seems to me urgent and vital. And completely unthinkable. For what is taking place here is a well-rehearsed performance in which everyone plays his role: the cantankerous 'traditionalists' talking of slavery, the smiling 'moderns' exalting sexual negritude, the enthusiastic audience, the condescending notabilities. This is play-acting, true to its illusory nature: the show being staged has no connection with the life unfolding beyond these walls.

Beyond these walls, a few hours away from Conakry, lie two countries in their death throes, Sierra Leone and Liberia, peopled with ghosts forever at one another's throats on soil crammed with gold and diamonds. Land where more mines are planted than crops. The play-acting makes it possible to forget this for as long as the show lasts. The intellectuals perform their verbal pirouettes, the leaders signal their approval by puffing up their greasy chops, the audience relishes the spicy witticisms ('Africa is an afrodisiac!' yells the Togolese writer). The organizer with her beetroot-coloured hair fidgets slightly on her chair, impatient to be mounted again by her Congolese friend. And at this very moment in a Liberian village a woman is being raped, a child's arm is being cut off. This is no mere probability. It is a statistical certainty.

The man gazing at the constellation of the Wolf was no dreamer. Quite simply, he knew that the viewpoint of the stars made it possible to tear down the walls behind which human beings hide for the satisfaction of remaining blind.

As I study the hall I reflect that it was this world here, this masquerade, that Elias detested the most. A world of which, at this moment, I am a part.

During the last days we spent in the furnace of Mogadishu, he must have understood perfectly that he was henceforth 'beyond redemption': useless now to the Soviets, who were making their catastrophic exit, but, above all, undesirable in his native Angola. For more than a week I did not see him, even in the distance, and I was comforted by this: I dreaded hearing him talk about the hopelessness of his situation. Not having seen him, I hoped he had succeeded in leaving Mogadishu by his own means. I remembered the thought that had crossed my mind from time to time in the past: why did he not give up all these increasingly absurd games of war and espionage and settle somewhere in the West? In truth, I still did not understand what Anna meant to him. Years later that handful of words he had exchanged with her in Moscow would come back to me: 'To go back . . . Back to Sarma . . .'

A new outburst of laughter in the hall. My neighbour on the platform nudges me with his elbow, and whispers a joke in my ear, the sense of which eludes me. I am back in the world Elias detested. The participants begin reading their texts about Africa, one after the other. So my own betrayal will have to come to this too.

V

The first impression: a flock of penguins, huddled close together, hiding their young ones inside the crowd. The men have their backs turned to the street, one of those streets which gunfire renders unusually noisy, with nowhere to hide. The plaintive voices of women can be heard, the wailing of children. Yes, penguins: the men's dark suits, the women's pale dresses. Everyone has tried to put on as many clothes as possible, despite the sun, so as not to have to leave them behind in this Mogadishu in flames. The crowd is pressed up against the closed gates of the American Embassy. They are the Soviets, the USSR Embassy has just been sacked and at this moment the looters are snatching up everything which may still be of use or could be sold. The houses in the capital have been dismembered like the carcasses of animals, down to their entrails, down to the scraping of the bones. The 'penguins' have already witnessed the knackers' handiwork and are massed together now, terrorized, pressed up against the American fortress.

I can see them from a car parked at the crossroads where a pile of plastic jerry-cans is burning. Beside me is Leonid, the doctor I met on the plane flying into Mogadishu. We are trying to negotiate with the representative of some armed band or other who dangles in front of us the possibility of evacuating the Embassy personnel by air. Several days ago Leonid operated on this Somali fighter's brother. The reward could therefore be this right of passage to the airport, to an aircraft coming from Addis Ababa. But the negotiations are dragging, the representative indicates that he would also like to receive some ready cash . . .

The sun is already heating the roof of the car appallingly. The crowd of 'penguins' on the other side of the road has become spotted with white: the women have covered their heads with panama hats or scarves, the men have donned the caps tourists wear. Indeed they look like an organized outing, an excursion to a site. I can make out the stooping figure of Vadim, who is talking to the ambassador, and a little to one side, outside the circle of 'penguins', Anna. Her gaze is directed towards the next street, where the ragged fighters are busy mounting a machine gun on a jeep. In the haste of the preparations and the flight, she must have forgotten that light white scarf that I have seen on her head on several occasions . . . From time to time she runs her hand through her hair, as if to drive away the heat.

Suddenly a lorry hurtles across the street, overturning the pile of jerry-cans on which the flames are dying down amid a stink of plastic. A burst of bullets rakes the enclosure surrounding the American Embassy, screams from women and oaths from men ring out in the crowd of 'penguins'. Someone starts rattling at the heavy gate that is still closed. Behind the houses with their windows blown out by explosions an eruption of black smoke arises and thickens. The air grows dark, the sun is eclipsed, then reappears, looking like a vast moon. Panic splits up the crowd into little groups, families, no doubt, then the din of a further explosion welds it together again with the animal fear of a tribe. In the car the Somali who was promising us a passage to the airport retracts. He must have realized that he lacked the time to extract wads of dollars from these terrorized foreigners. It seems easier to go off and loot a villa. Leonid insists, raises his voice. He is disfigured by tears, the weeping sickness he contracted one day in the mountains to the north of Kabul. He proposes a price to the Somali, gets out of the car, goes to report to the ambassador. I station myself in front of the vehicle so as to reduce the temptation for our saviour to do a runner. There are fresh explosions beyond the row of houses, the thump of mortar fire. In the middle of the crowd of bodies pressed together I notice the face of a very small child, who smiles at me, then hides, then reappears . . .

The roar from an artillery piece in the distance at first prevents me from understanding the argument that suddenly erupts within the group. In fact, it is one man yelling his head off. He is thickset, dressed in a velvet suit, his brow dripping with sweat. He seems first to be barking, then spluttering threats, while pointing his finger at Vadim. The latter backs away in the face of these violent attacks, mumbling excuses. They have separated from the crowd and are speaking louder, I finally grasp the reason for the confrontation. The man in the velvet suit is accusing Vadim of having left a computer behind at the embassy as well as (he emits a viperish hiss) a briefcase containing 'top-secret' diskettes . . . 'Just you wait! Back in Moscow we'll take good care of you. And as for your diplomatic passport, you can chuck that down the pan straight away! And let me point out that your wife had access to that computer, too . . .'

Anna, who has joined them, hears these last few words and tries to explain that, amid all the shooting, in a building on fire, there was no time to go and open the safe and take out the briefcase in question. The man feels caught out by this observation for he is the one, given his function, who should have rescued these 'top-secret' diskettes. But he is already fabricating an alibi for himself, looking for scapegoats. 'Just you wait! Back in Moscow heads will roll. Just you wait. Expect the worst. I'm warning you . . .'

A figure I do not recognize at once: a man dressed in a simple T-shirt and jeans. Elias. He must have been standing a couple of yards behind me, beside the car. He has heard everything. 'What's the combination for the safe?' he asks, addressing the man in the velvet suit. 'Why? What do you mean? Do you expect me . . .' The man's voice is choked. 'The combination?' repeats Elias more softly, looking at Vadim, who turns away slightly. Anna swiftly reels off a string of figures. An explosion very close at hand deafens us, the crowd of 'penguins' utters a howl. I have time to see Elias offering the driver a fistful of notes. The car drives off.

A continuous drumming of fists on the steel of the gate. Then an amazing lull, as if an armistice had finally been agreed. Unless it's the hour of prayer. The setting sun is still burning hot but will rapidly sink into the equatorial night. The smoke has already filled the city with an oily, suffocating dusk.

The car returns at this moment. What will stay with me of that scene is its bizarrely slow-motion pace, the cause of which I do not yet understand. Yes, the steps Elias takes, as if in a time warp. He goes up to the man in the velvet suit, hands him the briefcase. Then, with equal slowness, he hands Anna a white scarf, the one she always covered her head with against the sun . . . He seems to be about to speak but the words forming on his lips are inaudible. I believe what he says is being drowned by the sudden grinding of the gate. Then by the shouts of the crowd moving forward, plunging into the American paradise that is now ajar.

The 'penguins' jostle one another, a woman's hysterical cry can be heard ('You've lost your sandal!'), the ambassador's voice trying to discipline this mad rush, to give it a little dignity. For it is the 'American imperialists', their eternal enemies, who are about to give them shelter. I just have time to note the farcical nature of the situation and to glimpse a woman's face in the middle of the crowd being sucked into the funnel of the gateway. This face, Anna, looking back several times and Vadim drawing her along by her arm. I glance behind me but I can no longer see Elias. Neither in the crowd, nor in the Somali's jeep . . .

'He's over there!' I recognize Leonid's voice. Elias is sitting down, his back against the wheel, his eyes open, his hands trailing on the ground. His left arm, from shoulder to wrist, is red. A great patch spreads over his T-shirt as well, on his belly . . . We lift him up, his head moves and he is still trying to speak. Then we notice that the gate has closed once more. Leonid yells, kicks against the steel. Two cars pass in the street. Bullets chip at the paintwork on the gate right by our heads.

*   *   *

A scrap of garden with trees nicked by shell splinters, a house transformed into a makeshift hospital, a butterfly (no, a hummingbird) beating against the glass of an oil lamp. The stink of a generator, the bitter acidity of dirty, bloody bodies and from time to time, like the reminder of an impossible world, the cool of the ocean breeze. The buzzing of flies in this 'operating theatre', the crunch of shattered phials under foot, the continual, monotonous groaning of the wounded and their families.

Leonid works, assisted by a Somali doctor who is very slowly chewing a ball of khat. The hummingbird, intoxicated by the light, spirals down towards the busy hands. Leonid knocks it aside as one would swat a mosquito. The bullets he extracts and tosses into a metal basin make a sound similar to that given off by melting ice. From time to time the explosions obliterate all sound, then the movements of the two doctors become invested with a hint of unreality. Leonid operates without weeping. And yet his tape recorder sleeps in the big knapsack thrown down beside the door . . . I study his face. No, the eyes are dry, just reddened with tiredness.

He straightens up, puts down the lancet, draws a sheet over the body. 'There's no way he could have set one foot in front of the other with the wounds he had . . .' he murmurs. His eyes stare at me without seeing me. For a fraction of a second I believe I have touched upon the truth of what has happened: the man who had reappeared before us, a black briefcase in his hand, was no longer alive, but moved forwards, remaining upright, propelled by a force which resided somewhere other than in the body which now lies beneath this sheet.

* * *

We spend a whole day driving round in the blazing trap that is Mogadishu. The fact of carrying a dead man sometimes helps us to pass through road blocks. Despite the violence of the slaughter, these mortal remains seeking burial inspire a distant echo of the sacred in the fighters. In some streets the smoke from the fires is so thick that we have to pause before moving on, not knowing what we shall see when the darkness clears. It could be that man whom a shell has welded to a wall in an incrustation of blood and torn garments. Or that child, which has made itself a little aeroplane from the blade of an electric fan and is playing at launching it in the middle of the gunfire. Or yet again, as in an appalling nightmare, the turret of a buried tank: our attempts to escape had led us into the area of the presidential palace, which was protected by these sunken tanks, transformed into artillery pieces. The gun barrel moves with a somnambulistic slowness, points at us, stops . . . We make a sharp U-turn and drive away, feeling on the backs of our necks the full weight of this weapon taking aim.

A helicopter passes in the sky. We know at once that this is the Americans evacuating their personnel – and the members of the Soviet Embassy – onto the aircraft carrier *Guam*. I remember Elias's words: 'You'll soon be best friends with the Americans . . .'

At nightfall our driver leaves us several miles north of Mogadishu. He tells us he has run out of petrol and we have run out of money to pay for his services . . . During the night Leonid goes off towards the harbour, hoping to find some means of getting us onto a boat. The fever that was beginning to shake me the previous day changes into a fit of the shivers, which I cannot throw off, even pressed against the wall of a block-house that still holds the heat of the day. I wrap myself in a tarpaulin sheet found among the carcasses of cars. For a moment my shivering calms down. I adjust the blanket on Elias's body then clasp his hand in mine. It seems icy to me but like that of a man who has come in from a winter night, from the great plains of snow. The borderline between his death and my life seems incredibly fine. The same sand, still warm, beneath our bodies. The same slightly ashen darkness of the ocean. The same receding banks of cloud in the sky. Never before have I felt the presence of an absent one so intensely.

Leonid returns. He has had the luck to meet the engineer from a small cargo boat, quite an elderly man who trained in the USSR. This nostalgia was not enough, however: he had to give him both our watches and the money found in the leather pouch Elias carried on his belt . . .

Our embarkation takes place amid the ferocious melee of people staking their all to survive. No priority for anyone, men push women aside, trample on children. Leonid goes first, gripping the top end of the blanket in which Elias's body is wrapped. What helps his progress is his weeping malady, which suddenly over-comes him again. Even in the midst of this throng, people stand aside from what they take to be a super-natural being, a young man with completely white hair, his features disfigured by sobbing. I find it difficult to follow him, breathless, my jaws clenched to stop my teeth chattering at each spasm of fever. A child clings to my jacket and is dragged through the crowd on the landing stage. 'You've got malaria!' Leonid shouts suddenly, as if this diagnosis could make my task easier.

We collapse at the stern of the boat in a seething mass of bodies, bundles, chests, ropes. The deck is covered in fine coal dust, which mingles with the white powder escaping from the sacks of flour being transported by half a dozen men as they brutally thrust aside the refugees and their wretched luggage. This loading reassures us a little: it is doubtless humanitarian aid that has been diverted and is due to be unloaded in a foreign port, along with ourselves.

At the end of the night the cargo boat attempts to berth. The outline of a jetty can be seen emerging from the darkness, a few lights . . . And then there are these interminable seconds when we are still moving forwards even though the boat's engines have already gone into reverse at full power. From the jetty a heavy machine gun is raking it with, one might say, the infantile glee of having found a target exposed, as if in a shooting gallery. The cries of those afraid of being killed are as always, more shrill than the moans of those who have just been hit. A wild-looking man approaches the deck-house, seeking refuge, sits down, spits blood. A woman beside me, all hunched up, scrapes patiently at the flaking paintwork on the coal-blackened deck. She will carry on with her demented activity throughout the day, as if to give just measure to the madness that surrounds us.

In the morning, travelling within a few miles of the

shore, we pass alongside fabulous gardens whose abundance cuts into the dry and ochreous line of the coast. Houses hidden in their greenery, hinting at shade and coolness. A town to the south of Mogadishu, Merca, no doubt. A paradise before the hell of a day baked by the sun and thirst.

An important day for both of us. We have to rid ourselves of our fear, the sentimentality of memories, of all notion of superiority in the face of this suffering human mass, this woman scratching at the flaking paintwork. We are all fraternally united by the spark of life that still glows in us all. And when, after another attempt at landing and more shooting, the people around us lie down on the deck, we do the same, pressed up against these emaciated bodies, protecting the body of Elias stretched out between us.

At the approach of night (our second night at sea), the boat sails further from the coast, then suddenly stops and, incredulous, we hear the engine wheezing as it slows down, then finally, and even more unbelievably, silence. Or rather the inhalations and exhalations of the heap of human beings on the deck, their groaning, murmuring, rustling. The night is perfectly calm, without any breeze, and these quiet voices filter out from the darkness with striking intimacy. My own breathing, made jerky by the fever, seems to me deafening. Leonid sits up, removes his headphones and in their susurration I recognize one of the tunes I know, which he listens to over and over again to struggle against his tears.

We do not know if the ship will move on and what its destination will be. This uncertainty no longer concerns us. We speak briefly about Elias and decide what we must now do. Leonid clears a way for himself, stepping over recumbent bodies, and disappears into the bowels of the ship. He returns quickly, laden with a heavy cast-iron cogwheel and an old, worn length of rope . . .

Elias's face, as we look at it for the last time, appears relaxed, like that of one asleep. I am afraid lest this body, in its blanket bound with ropes, might look like a parcel. But its outline is more reminiscent of a carved block of stone. To the foot of this block Leonid fastens the cogwheel.

The level of the cargo boat's afterdeck is a few feet above the water. We lay out the body along the steel gunwale, then rise upright above him, only able to honour him by standing clumsily to attention thus, among passengers who lie, sit and stand. The silence of a moment ago has given way to an increasingly violent hubbub. People are remonstrating with the crew members, hammering on the wheelhouse door. While the boat was under way it mattered little to them where it was bound for, since we were travelling away from death. Now death assumes the face of this calm, moonless night, without a breath of air. Immobility, thirst, this boat stock-still amid the murky darkness of sky and ocean. I see a man with a long knife in his hand slicing through the crowd to reach a sailor, who points an automatic pistol at him; it is strangely small, almost a toy. Two other men grapple with one another, yelling, thrusting one another against a metal companionway. The weeping of the children blends together, for a moment, into a shrill chorus, then only the woman scraping at the deck seems totally separate from the madness of the people whose shouting is an attempt to keep death at bay. I see that, in fact, she is obstinately cleaning the dirty surface: a very smooth little square is already gleaming beneath her fingers.

Without conferring, Leonid and I pause for a breathing space, a moment of silence. He, his face streaming with tears that he no longer even notices, myself, attempting to contain the fever that freezes me. The woman cleaning the deck is slowly drawing closer to the place where we threw down our gear.

The question must have been asked once already for the chairman seems to be repeating it with the slow insistence one adopts when faced with a foreigner who is not quick on the uptake. I really only gather my wits at the moment when this voice with carefully enunciated syllables is uttering the final words. An embarrassed silence. I rouse myself from my memories, encounter the looks, amused or uneasy, of the other participants in the round-table discussion, the chairman's frozen smile . . . The Togolese writer, inexhaustible this evening, saves the situation: 'I'd like to take advantage of my Russian colleague's confusion to tell you that, during his travels in the East, Flaubert saw nothing shocking in a woman profiting from her body with total freedom. In African women this utilitarian attitude is very widespread . . .' The debate resumes, the chairman is visibly relieved. This fragment sticks in my mind: 'With total freedom'. The freedom of the African woman selling her body . . .

Just now, when I felt I was still present in that room, a hardened, trenchant indignation tore at nerves within me that I had thought long since blanketed in indifference. I loathed that gang of 'international bureaucrats', sitting there in the front row after a week of palavers and meals in a luxury hotel. I remarked to myself what

I had had occasion to observe twenty years earlier: how many children could be saved for the price of just one of those suits each of these monstrous Africans was wearing? I loathed the intellectual geisha girls, performing their 'afrodisiac Africa' routine for these blasé spectators, instead of being up in arms. They were carving up the continent just like that photo I had seen in a book as a child long ago: a dismembered elephant. Its head, the trunk, the body, the legs . . . Everyone got their share that evening. The bureaucrats, the intellectuals, the audience who, for want of anything better, were laughing at these grandstanding writers' banter. And even that organizer with her locks dyed beetroot, she had contrived to carve herself a portion of flesh, the body of the young Congolese . . .

At a certain moment the sight of their faces became too painful for me. I hastened to plunge back into that terrible night in Somalia, compounded of massacre, screaming and thirst, but where nevertheless I managed to breathe. I knew that past could only end in death for some, flight for others, and for the two of us a long, chaotic return (a week convalescing in Addis Ababa), a return to a homeland, to that USSR which, by the end of the same year, would no longer exist. And yet on this boat, adrift on an ocean at night, the sovereign truth of life broke through: the certainty that the passing of a man who loved does not signify the death of the love he carried within him.

The violence of the voices flayed by despair, the movement of shadows through the tangle of bodies, two laments intermingled, that of a mother and of her child.

And that woman still scraping at the deck's dirty surface. Slowly she draws closer to the place where we threw down our gear . . .

The sound erupts suddenly. Powerfully vibrant organ music, interwoven with violins. The woman must have turned up the volume of the tape recorder Leonid left beside our bags. She did it with the same action as her scraping, turning it up fully. Consciously or not? With the inspired awareness of madness, let us say. For only this tragic and triumphant thunder is capable of cutting through the madness that has taken hold of the boat. People freeze. Voices fall silent. The heady outburst of organ music protects the boat's solitude.

Elias's body disappears slowly. The water is so calm that this human shape looks as if it were rising amid the stars, into a sky deeper than the sky.

When the music stops, very clearly, amid absolute silence, a child's sigh can be heard.